In the Footsteps of the Silver King

Paul Kareem Tayyar

Spout Hill Press

For my Mother and Father, and for Father Vernon Ruland, Father Timothy Doyle, and Father James Conway

Acknowledgements

A short excerpt of this novel was published in *The Santa Monica Review*, 2005.

Prologue
My Father Rode Horses and Stole Cars

My father was always unimpressed with the great epic heroes of world literature. Sinbad the Sailor should have figured out after the first shipwreck—and certainly no later than the second—that he would have been better off staying at home and watching the Game of the Week than embarking on any more journeys. Odysseus was overrated, a hubristic sea-captain who seemed best at getting the men in his charge killed in the most brutally awful ways, and who, when it came down to it, was far happier being stuck on Calypso's island than he let on. "After all," my father used to say, "even Tom Hanks in *Castaway* figured out how to build a raft, and he was a FedEx employee, instead of a guy with half of Mt. Olympus on his side." Gilgamesh was a momma's boy, Beowulf a meathead, Robin Hood a communist. When, on one particularly memorable occasion, my father came home from work to find me reading the final chapters of Tolkien's *The Lord of the Rings*, he shook his head and said, "Are those guys still walking across the Shire? They've been doing that since 1922."

I always used to get a kick out of this, especially because, when actually comparing such supposedly mythic figures to my actual father, they *did* always seem to come up short. Indeed, I don't remember Beowulf ever single-handedly turning over a four-door Cadillac sedan when its now absent-driver had decided to park his car in our designated apartment parking space, nor could I remember

Gilgamesh successfully eating 25 Pink's Hot Dogs on a particularly warm Los Angeles afternoon after my parents had taken me on a trip to the La Brea Tar Pits. I certainly knew that, whatever else Odysseus' strengths may have been, if he had that much trouble finding his way back to Ithaca even with the goddess Athena riding shotgun for most of his adventures, there is no way he would have been able to drive my mother, my best friend Danny and I back through the Grand Tetons in the middle of the worst snowstorm in thirty years without the benefit of working headlights or functional tire chains.

My father mopped the floor with those legends, plain and simple. But as I got a little older, I began to wonder if his animosity towards those "guys," as he used to call them, didn't also have more than a little to do with just how much like him they actually were. Like my father, they were possessed with such reserves of unimaginable good fortune that it often seemed as if their greatness was less a matter of divine providence and more a simple case of pure dumb luck, and, also like my father, they were rarely, if ever, satisfied with the considerable servings of amazing experience God (or the gods) had chosen to grant them. It became funnier and funnier to me over the years—if not, in the words of young Alice as she moved through Wonderland, "curiouser and curiouser"—that Sinbad the Sailor's wandering spirit and faraway eyes got on my father's nerves, or that he could never understand why Odysseus found it necessary, upon returning to Ithaca, to almost immediately set sail again. After all, that was my father's M.O. as well. He was a man forever on the move, certain in the way that only the truly charmed can be that they will always make it through unscathed.

But I am getting ahead of myself. I guess I should start at the beginning, or, perhaps, even before that, considering that to understand the story I am about to tell it is necessary not only to know a little bit more about my father, but to also have some sense of the country that produced him. Therefore, let me start with a brief snapshot of both the Iran of my father's childhood and a short chronicling of some of my father's greatest hits.

There were taxicabs in the city with goats strapped to the tops of the roofs. There were two-story houses whose sole source of water was the three-thousand-year old well in the middle of their gardens. There was my father on a horse his grandfather owned, racing it through the kind of landscape I have only seen in black and white photographs, old David Lean films, or the dreams I often used to have when I thought my father, after having had a particularly terrible fight with my mother, would not be coming home again. There was my father in a car he had heisted from his father's estate, a gesture of repudiation towards a man who ran his family the way the Shah ran the country: with sustained, devastating cruelty. If my mother's teenage years of growing up in Los Angeles were defined by Civil Rights, The Beatles, Cesar Chavez, and the Lakers losing to the Boston Celtics, my father's early years in Shiraz were defined by the secret police, Muhammad Ali prizefights on tape-delay, the palpably dangerous tension between secularism and Islam, and so many car thefts that it had become my father's own private ritual—he stole them as often as his countrymen knelt towards Mecca in recognition of their Muslim faith.

I was good at it too, he would say. *I should have taught you how to do it when you were young enough not to know any better.*

And the truth was that if you could consider stealing cars from the city's aristocratic rich a type of faith, my father's faith, as he would later say, was a lot more satisfying. His faith went from 0 to 60 in 8 seconds flat. His faith took him out past the desert flats of Persepolis and onto the highways of Western Esfahan, leaving clouds of diesel-dust swirling around the shrines of martyrs whose names he had memorized in school. My father's faith was his and his alone. You want Allah? Allah was in the transmission of a black-market 1953 Chevrolet convertible, in the whitewalls of a BMW that looked like something James Bond would later drive. *Believe me, I didn't need to pray five times a day for miracles*, he'd say. *I'd simply hot-wire a black Mercedes and be a vital part of a fuel-injected resurrection for the rest of the afternoon.*

And then he'd smile. The smile that for twenty years got him out of trouble with my mother. Whatever he had done—and he did a lot—that smile was like an American Express Black Card, the type that only billionaires are given, Bill Gates and Warren Buffet and Michael Jordan, the type that when you flash it they don't need to call your bank to make sure you're good for whatever you have decided to purchase.

It now makes sense why he loved American action films: *Die Hard, Cliffhanger, Lethal Weapon, Bullitt, The French Connection, Payback*. On some level, those films—and their leading men—must have reminded my father of himself. My father's life had been its own adventure flick, though rather than culminating in the ultimate defeat of the bad guys, be they cops-gone-bad, Apartheid sympathizers or German hostage-takers, his narrative arc was composed of a series of increasingly unlikely, miraculous even, escapes.

Over the years, from sources ranging from the comically secondhand (gas station attendants who had fixed the automobiles of men who had once worked with guys who had known my father a decade earlier) to the wholly reliable (me, my mother, my grandparents, close family friends) there had been stories of such strange, unimaginable grandeur that, by my early twenties, I had come to see my father as a Middle Eastern Rasputin, or, for those unfamiliar with one of the more eerily superhuman figures in Russian history, a non-smoking, non-drinking, non-guitar playing Persian Keith Richards. Simply put, my father was a man who, as Mike Myers famously said in that classic of B-level American cinema, *Wayne's World*, "couldn't be killed by conventional weapons."

A brief history of my father's near misses:

1. Climbs down a well at six years old—*climbs*, not falls—and not immediately realizing the stupidity of the decision, decides to play at its waterless bottom for several hours rather than screaming for help. By nightfall, hungry, and limited by the darkness that has inevitably shrouded the ancient construction, he begins his long, slow climb back to middle earth, cutting his hands on the jagged rope so terribly he will later require several stitches in both palms.

2. On a day trip with his family at eight years old (he and his brother, two years younger, have been told by their parents they are going on a picnic), my father wanders off into the surrounding clearing, slipping between the ropes of an

11

obviously private premises, to chase rattlesnakes and to build sandcastles in the dirt. He is shaken from this brief bliss of childhood pastoral by a voice on a loudspeaker, muffled by the cheapness of its electrical feed, yelling at him in a staccato Farsi that (to anyone who has ever been cursed out in that ancient, beautifully poetic language, can be aesthetically thrilling and unbelievably frightening), "he'd better get his ass out of there ASAP," only to have that admittedly urgent threat be immediately followed by a concussive force not five feet from him of such strength that he was certain, as he later told my mother, that a bomb had been dropped on his head.

It hadn't been. Not exactly.

What *had* been dropped was a man—to be followed, within a matter of seconds, by many, many more men— parachuting from the sky. When my father's family had told him that they were going on a picnic, they didn't mention that it was a picnic to be held at a military air show, with one of the main events being a massive sky-diving exhibition performed by the Army's Air Corps.

My father had wandered—in what I now see as a rather fitting metaphor for much of his adult life—into a restricted area where, upon successfully trespassing and intently chasing rattlesnakes for several minutes, he calmly settled down to the business at hand of building the most accomplished, ornate series of sandcastles the city of Shiraz had ever seen. For obvious reasons, no visual record of the sand castles exists, other than in my father's own recollection of the afternoon. But as he later told me, *the guys who built Versailles would have hung their heads in shame.* And as for my father's response to the unexpected realization he was about to be killed by one of many nameless, and of course, blameless, paratroopers trying to land without incident, he and his brother left their beloved sandcastles to their fates and sprinted, in the most jagged, serpentine of fashions, in between the falling men like frightened, retreating soldiers who suddenly realize they have wandered into a field surrounded by embedded snipers.

3. At ten years old, he is electrocuted when his electrically powered toy helicopter, a gift from an uncle who would come to regret purchasing it for my father, lands in the pool of a neighbor's yard. My father dislodges the metal pole upon which his family's living room curtains rest, and attempts to use the pole as a rescue device for his Navy chopper which has gone down behind enemy lines (this was no exaggeration: he hated his neighbors with the passion of a fiercely nationalistic soldier). When I asked my father about this particular incident several years back, he only offered the following understated response: "I still made it to school the next day."

4. Fast forward to 1976. My father is twenty-three years old, working the graveyard shift at an Arco Station in the Tenderloin District of San Francisco thanklessly manning the register for a place that would be robbed three times during his first six months on the job; my mother is twenty-five, pregnant, working as a nurse at San Francisco General, a hospital teeming with overworked nurses and doctors alike, the strong ones pulling double-shifts and still keeping their hearts, minds, and spirits intact, the weak ones pulling double-shifts and resorting to methamphetamines, binge-drinking, and sports gambling to see themselves through the

admittedly high-pressure occupation they have chosen. My parents own an ancient Chevrolet Impala, the kind that guzzled enough gas to justify our nation's invasions of some oil-rich Middle Eastern nation-state, the kind with more steel surrounding its chassis than the Batmobile.

My father is driving, my mother is dozing in the passenger seat, later saying that Stevie Wonder's song, "If It's Magic," an almost a capella track from that year's multi-platinum, Grammy-winning release by the man who owned the airwaves during the second half of the 1970s, was playing in her head. "It was the only album we owned at the time, and I used to play it nonstop around the apartment," my mother would say nostalgically. There is an out-of-operation yellow city bus barreling down Eddy Street at Nascar-level speeds, the driver drunk, the collision inevitable.

The police estimate my parents' car flipped over at least twenty-five times. The roof collapses, the engine, as if it were a piece of tempered glass, shatters, the two back windows blow out, sending shards across the back seat, a few stray ones into my mother's scalp. My mother has hit her head on the dashboard and is knocked cold, her body curled into the fetal position, an unconscious reaction of maternal protection that is symbolic of the heroic levels of love and sacrifice with which she raised me, her body in the earliest stages of shock.

My father, unharmed, pulls my mother from the car, cracks his own neck a few times, and has to be restrained by several passersby from attacking the barely conscious bus driver. The ambulance takes my mother to the hospital, my father goes to work, putting on the sweater his mother had knit him for his eighteenth birthday, the last birthday he would ever spend with her, to cover the blood that had emanated from a small cut above my mother's left eye and splashed across his collar and right sleeve like the brushstrokes of a late period De Kooning painting.

5. At twenty-seven my father, along with our downstairs neighbor Bob, a borderline felon and all-out deadbeat, on a trip to the beach both men's families had taken—there are photographs of me from this afternoon, my ever-present red cap on my head, still mysteriously without eyebrows of any kind (I would not have them for another six years, until the age of ten, when even I was beginning to wonder what the hell was going on), playing in the sand with Bob's daughter, a girl who last I heard was doing three to five for assaulting her live-in boyfriend with the heel of one of the dress pumps that she used to wear on stage, grinding away with a boa constrictor for the all-night truckers and railroad men in a Coolidge Springs strip palace a few miles west of the Salton Sea, totally oblivious to the fact that neither my father nor Bob had been spotted for the better part of an hour, though they had promised their respective wives they were just going into the water to do a bit of bodysurfing. Naturally, that bit of bodysurfing took them so many miles out the Coast Guard had to be called in, the rescue men coming upon two heads bobbing in deep water, my father's still vibrant voice as even as it always was, Bob's eyes closed (he was passed out from exhaustion), my father supporting the both of them in the riptide they had been caught within. That night, the three of us sitting in front of the television set, watching the season finale of *Magnum, P.I.*, my father said, "I should have let him drown. It would have been a favor to his family." Bob's wife,

who left with all four kids six months later after Bob attacked her with a hunting knife, if caught in an honest moment, probably would have agreed.

6. At thirty-six, my father's car is found totaled and abandoned in a ravine off the 405 freeway. The driver's side window has been shattered, the trunk is now in the backseat, but the briefcase my father always carries is mysteriously absent, as is, equally mysteriously, my father, considering that the police can't imagine somebody walking away from such a crash. It is rather likely they mean "walking away" in a dual sense: "walking away" as in surviving unharmed a crash like this, and "walking away" as in actually *leaving* the scene of a crash like this. No witnesses to the accident come forward, occurring as it did, we come to find out, twelve hours later when my father returns home, some time after midnight, and because the nearest exit to the crash was located in the city of Irvine, a city unmatched in its people's almost complete disengagement with the larger world.

Nevertheless, my mother spends the rest of the evening making frantic phone calls to family and friends, checking the local news for reports of a Middle Eastern man bleeding from the head and suffering from an apparent bout of total amnesia, pausing during commercials to tell me, "Darnit, Patrick. Don't ever do this to the woman you love, okay?" as she fixes my hair, asks me if I'm hungry, and makes sure that all of my homework has been completed in time for tomorrow's classes. When my father finally makes it home, casually unlocking the door, leaving his briefcase in the entrance closet, and then saying hello to us, my mother mutes the television with the remote control, certain that some impassioned explanation—revelation, even, considering it had been almost an entire twenty-four hours since the accident—was forthcoming.

Instead what he gave us was, "Hi guys. What's for dinner?"

In a state of collective shock, neither my mother nor I say anything for the better part of a minute, before my mother, calmly, her voice betraying only the slightest waver of desperation, asks, "Hassan, what happened?"

"What do you mean?"

It is at this moment that, were there any recorded audio of the moment for future generations of dysfunctional American families, the tape would have segued into several minutes of screeching, static, and the apparent, but not definitive, sounds of household materials being hastily, angrily rearranged, with only fragments of my parents' exchange, as if their discussion were taking place with them located on opposite sides of a drive-through call-box at a neighborhood McDonalds, surviving:

"—I had to get to work."

"You couldn't have ca—"

"Why do you always worry so much?"

"—kidding me?"

What the surviving fragments of tape reveal is a man so consumed with the project he was immersed in at work that a serious automobile accident was not reason enough to wait for the police or to, at the very least, telephone his family to inform them of what had happened. My father, as was one of his talents, chose Door Number Three when only two doors were visible to everyone else in the television audience: he took his briefcase from the wreckage, walked to the yellow call box that, with the omnipresence of cellular phones in Southern California, is now as much a thing of the past as the drive-in movie theater, and telephoned a cab. He was at work, holed up in his office, working on formulas that would lead to the breakthrough the software he had been assigned to develop needed to become operable, within the hour.

If there were a casting call for a real-life equivalent of Sylvester Stallone's Rocky Balboa, a man with both the strange, if not pathological, desire to continue placing himself in the most obviously, immediately violent of circumstances, long past when even the most believing of his fans had ceased being willing to cheer on such near-suicidal tendencies, and the clearly unexplainable talent for then emerging from such multi-round trauma not only unscathed but triumphant, I would certainly be inclined to nominate my father. His life, to this point, has been a pageant of the bizarre and the life-threatening, yet he is, more than any other person I have met in my life, completely unfazed by the events of his past, never pausing for the briefest of reflections as to why, for instance, he has been in, to date, twelve car accidents, or why he has *twice* been chased by packs of wild dogs who have broken free of their rickety fences in small Texas towns while taking his unusually long walks around the neighborhood of the Lone Star town he inhabited in the 1990s, making money hand over fist for a rising tech firm, driving his second wife so crazy with worry she once telephoned my mother for emotional support and commiseration. My mother, perhaps the only other woman in the world who could truly understand the woman's pain, stayed on the phone for the better part of an hour, telling her that no, things were most likely not going to be okay, but he would, as he always had, certainly make it home alive.

I offer this snapshot of my father not as indictment but as celebration. Indeed, the years have made it clear to me that my father's life was the central inspiration for my decision to become a writer. I have found that writing, especially the magic realist novels and poems which have become my bread and butter, has come to replace the adventures, the sheer sense of the unreal, that my father took with him when he moved back to his homeland. He is, to quote the words of Hunter Thompson's immortal, ever-stoned alter-ego Raoul Duke, spoken while watching his oversized, maniacal, ethical, fiercely intelligent, tough-as-nails, self-destructive sidekick Samoan lawyer Dr. Gonzo, "one of God's own prototypes, never even considered for mass production." He is a good man still waiting to return to the planet he is suited for—and, as is quite likely, should such a planet not exist—to forcibly change the landscape of this planet to make it, finally, suitably inhabitable for him.

Or at least he was.

On the morning of June 5, 2009, I received a phone call from my father's second wife, Nazim, informing me that he had died peacefully in his sleep, hours after the two of them had stayed up late watching a pirated (in Iran, everything worth watching or listening to is pirated) DVD copy of *The Sting*—my father's favorite movie, which centers on Paul Newman and Robert Redford's attempts to avenge the murder of their best friend by swindling the gangster who ordered the hit out of his entire fortune—in their second-floor living room. I was something more than merely surprised. I was downright stunned. In fact, I think my genuine sadness was, in those first few hours after receiving the news, trumped by a kind of disappointment, as if my father owed it to himself and to those he loved to have died the way he lived: while walking across yet another tightrope of his own devising.

Years earlier my father had raved about the benefits of living in an authoritarian country: *the nineteen-year-old kids on the street have everything months before America has it. The new Mac computers, pop records that won't hit the airwaves for another year in the west, guns that will shoot through the guy robbing you, the walls of your house, the window of the getaway car he's got idling out front, and the skull of the ex-revolutionary he's got manning the wheel.* And at the top of the list was the ready availability of the movies he loved. And it was good to know that *The Sting* was the last film that he ever watched, as it championed everything that mattered most to him in life: a David vs. Goliath narrative, wonderful music, and a laid-back, laconic, devil-may-care humor that nobody did better than Paul Newman in his prime. For the next week, I found myself imagining him as he must have been that night: sitting on the couch and eating a meal of steak kabob, saffron rice, and a healthy serving of ghormeh sabzi, laughing when Newman's Henry Gondorff blusters and cheats his way into the rigged card game on the 20th Century Limited, nodding sagely as Redford's Johnny Hooker tells Gondorff he wants to play the big con on the crooked, murderous Doyle Lonnegan because he "doesn't know enough about killing to kill him," and clapping his hands, once, during the film's coda, when Hooker refuses his share of the cut—this was always about friendship, not money for him—and walking off into the darkness of prohibition era Chicago with Gondorff by his side.

What surprised me most, however, was that Nazim informed me that, though my father was to be buried in a quiet ceremony in the town that he was born in (Shiraz, the City of Poets), he had left a package for me that would be arriving by airmail within the month. She could not be any more precise: this was still the Middle East, after all, and I was living in America. In other words, that these two regions even agreed to ship each other's mail was a matter of no small significance, considering that the last thirty years had been spent largely riling up their own respective bases by calling for the eradication—or at least the possibility of such an act—of the other country. We were still, even three decades later, living in the shadow of the 1979 American Embassy hostage crisis, which meant that every time I picked up the phone to dial his number I figured there were probably coffee-drinking CIA analysts pulling all-night shifts at Langley intently listening in on our discussions of why the U.S. National Soccer team was still decades away from winning a World Cup, and that it would likely be as long before the Iranian National Basketball team resembled something other than the traveling dunces that the Harlem Globetrotters beat up and embarrassed night after night, year after year, in front of adoring and complicit crowds.

I told her I would keep an eye out for it, and went about setting up a memorial service for my father to be held in Laguna Beach, at a park where there were always soccer games going on Saturday and Sunday afternoons. I made the necessary phone calls and placed obituaries in the San Francisco Chronicle, the Los Angeles Times, and the Orange County Register. It was a lovely service. My mother and her entire side of the family came to say their goodbyes, and friends of his I didn't know existed—gas station mechanics from South Central, strawberry pickers from Fountain Valley, artists from the Mission District in San Francisco—came to pay their respects, and to tell me how much they had heard about me over the years.

The package arrived the day after the memorial.

Chapter 1
An Accidental Thief in the Night

My father's letter was written in such a clipped,
understated style that for a moment I thought he had
stumbled upon a lost letter of Ernest Hemingway's and was
simply forwarding it to me for safekeeping. Nevertheless,
here were its contents:

Go and find my silver medal. Bring it to Iran and bury it with
my tomb. You'll know where to find it. Say hi to everyone.

Not exactly Paul's Letter to the Corinthians or Lincoln's
Gettysburg Address, but it was certainly in keeping with my
father's less-is-more style.

The medal to which my father was referring was the
World Games silver medal that he received by being a
goalkeeper on the Iranian National Team, a squad which lost
in one of the most famous international championship
matches of the decade, 4-3, to a British team so stocked with
superstars that there were First League stalwarts who never
got off the bench. Other than a small suitcase full of clothes,
a used copy of the *Collected Poems of Hafiz*, and the pair of
Adidas cleats my father had worn throughout that legendary
tournament, the medal was all he had brought to America
when he first arrived at San Francisco International Airport.

We had never—at least that I could recall—talked
about his experiences as a soccer star. Rather, his attention
was most often concentrated on Dan Rather's reading of the

Evening News, a program that most likely centered on the Watergate redux of the Iran-Contra Crisis and the gradual deterioration of communist strength in Eastern Europe. Indeed, had my father never written this posthumously mailed letter, I would likely have forgotten that the medal even existed at all. I thought often of my father's soccer exploits—I still followed international soccer closely, I think, as a kind of quiet, personal appreciation for what he had accomplished in the game—but almost never of its physical rewards. He hadn't kept his jerseys, his game shorts, or shin guards, nor did he have framed in our living room a poster advertising that greatest of Middle Eastern teams. To have left Iran in the mid-1970s to immigrate to America was akin to having gone to colonize the planet Mars. Or to paraphrase Springsteen: you took what you could carry, and you left the rest.

That being said, my father had asked something of me, perhaps for the only time in his life, and there was never a question for me as to what I would do: I would ensure the medal would be returned to its first and rightful owner, even though, as had always been the case, my father assumed a level of talent on the part of his son that I did not actually possess. I had no idea who might have the medal. But I figured I would start with the person I thought was the likeliest to know about the medal's whereabouts: Crazy Dave Grushecky, part-time welder, part-time deep-sea fisherman, all-time wild man, and most importantly for my purposes, my father's best friend.

Crazy Dave, my mother once said, got involved in deep-sea fishing for the same reason most American men get involved with any adventurous pastime: to escape the day-today tedium of married life. Thus, his decisions to fish off the coasts of Catalina and the Channel Islands as frequently as he did was motivated more by a desire to avoid the tasks your average American husband is expected to perform on Sunday afternoons (mowing the lawn, fixing the rusted hinges of the aged garage door, helping ferry the kids to soccer games and Confirmation practice) than it was a special fondness or emotional connection with the sea. In this respect, at least, Dave was exactly like my father, save for the fact that we didn't have a lawn (we had lived in an apartment building) or a garage door, and I had retired early from both soccer and Catholicism.

After a quick call to my mother checking to see if she knew where Dave might be was unsuccessful—"that's a name I haven't heard in years," she said—I knew it was time to play amateur detective, something that Google had made almost ridiculously easy and convenient over the course of the past several years: you could channel your inner Sam Spade without ever having to leave the comfort of your living room, so long as it was internet-enabled.

However, while contemporary cultural critics, media pundits, and academic researchers would have you believe we are living in the Age of the Internet, a post-privacy era where everything—photographs, diaries, friendships, break-ups—are experienced almost exclusively online, the truth is that there are individuals, tens of millions of them, in fact, who leave no online footprint, their names registering nary a blip when typed into the Google search engine. That Dave should have been just such a ghost was hardly a surprise; judging by the two or three times in my life when I actually spent time with him—the last time being when the three of us, Dave, my father, and I, went to watch the Dodgers beat the San Francisco Giants at Chavez Ravine a few days after the L.A. Riots ended, smoke still lingering in the air, the town's massively diverse populace attempting to suture up its still-infected wounds by enjoying our national pastime. Dave had broken into a surprisingly beautiful a capella "This Land Is Your Land" after the last out of the ninth was registered that had everybody in our seating area transfixed and nodding their heads. Even at fifteen years old I knew this was a guy living in an era that had not existed since the days of Buffalo Bill and Jesse James. He was the type of American male that never went to the doctor, knew how to clean and load his gun, and who believed that church was the place you went only if a buddy was getting married or a buddy had died (which, in Dave's mind, meant basically the same thing).

Instead I walked down to the corner of Broadway and Magnolia, a few blocks from my house in Long Beach, and stepped into what might have been the last remaining phone booth in all of L.A. County: I was an out-of-time Clark Kent, thumbing through the yellow pages for an ex-Marine who might or might not be alive.

He was. And he still lived where he always had: at the top of Bunker Hill in downtown Los Angeles, a section of the City of Angels that the new-age developers had not been able to pry away from the boho-squatters, ex-soldiers, and would-be artists who called these aged streets their home. Bunker Hill was the L.A. of John Fante, Jake Gittes, and Philip Marlowe, a place where no good deed ever went unpunished, and where men still took buses to their jobs each and every morning, and the corner grocer would usually front you some food on credit if he liked the way you shook his hand. I dialed the number. A woman's voice answered on the second ring.

"Hello?"

"Hello. Is Dave Grushecky there?"

"No, he isn't. May I ask who's speaking?"

"Yes, my name is Patrick Karimi. I am—"

"Patrick! Oh, it's wonderful to hear from you. God, how long has it been? How is your father?"

"He passed away last week," I answered.

There was a long pause.

"I'm so sorry to hear that. What happened?"

"He had a heart attack in his sleep," I said. "He didn't suffer."

"Your father was a good man, Patrick. I always loved seeing him. Dave is going to be devastated."

"Actually, that's why I was calling. Dave may have some information on something that belonged to my father that I am trying to track down. Do you know when he'll be back?"

"Probably not for a couple of hours. He's at the fair with some friends of his. He said they had some business to take care of," she said, sounding confused. "I don't know what it could be. We were at the fair last night."

"Does he have a cell phone?" I asked.

"Yes, do you want the number?"

Before hanging up, Janie had informed me that, for the first time in its eighty-plus year history, the Los Angeles County Fair was being held not outside the city proper in neighboring Pomona, but right in the heart of downtown.

"You're kidding," I said.

"No, the city council thought it would be a good test run for the football stadium they're going to build down there." And then, after a pause, she added, "Good luck. The parking is a nightmare."

I dialed the cell phone number and, after a few seconds, the sound of a man's voice was barely audible above the sound of carnival music playing in the background. I half-wondered if Dave was riding a Ferris Wheel as he answered the phone. After a minute or so of trying to establish a working connection, Dave bellowed:

"Hey there, Patrick! It's good to hear from you, buddy. Listen, I'm out here at the fair right now. Are you in the area? Come on out and I'll meet you. We can talk about the old times! I'll meet you in an hour out in front of the Shake Shack near the bumper cars."

He hung up. Well, I said to myself, it looks like I'm going to the Los Angeles County Fair for the first time in twenty years.

I walked back home, grabbed the keys to my car and prepared to hit the road, which, at 4:30pm on a Thursday in Southern California meant a ten to fifteen mile per hour crawl up the 710 and then the 5 freeways, listening to local sports radio touts alternately praise and curse the Lakers (depending on how they were playing), right-wing talk radio hacks preaching the Gospel of Necessary Tax Cuts and a Return to Traditional Family Values (code for No Gays Allowed), and FM rock and roll stations that had collectively decided nothing of musical note was recorded after Van Halen's 1984 hit "Jump," when David Lee Roth ruled the rock landscape like a latter-day Robert Plant. In other words, the twenty miles between Long Beach and downtown Los Angeles was going to take at least an hour and a half. That's just the way it was. Had Lancelot and his crew come to realize the Holy Grail was hidden somewhere in Tinseltown, they would have run out of gas halfway up Sunset Boulevard. After all, there was a reason Burt Reynolds' road trip classics of the late 1970s and early 1980s were filmed in the still largely rural south and not the freeway-congested west: there was no such thing as an open road out here. Even Huck Finn would have fled to Portland.

I spent the drive channel-surfing on the radio, listening to fragments of songs I liked—Springsteen's "Born to Run," Prince's "Let's Go Crazy," Blondie's "Dreaming"— and dropping in and out of talk-radio monologues that, at the very least, kept my attention with their verbosity and their inviolable assurance in the righteousness of their opinions:

"Magic Johnson is the greatest Laker in NBA history."

"There will never be another Sandy Koufax."

"Villaraigosa is a chump."

"One good earthquake and we'll all be dead anyway."

"Where's Tom Bradley when you need him?"

"John Wooden was to college basketball what Abe Lincoln was to politics."

"Obama didn't deserve his Nobel Peace Prize."

"Neither did Al Gore."

"Bill Clinton did more for World Peace than any President since John Kennedy."

"Bush wasn't as bad as everyone thought he was."

"The internet is dulling our brains."

"The four scariest letters in America? F.E.M.A."

"The Dodgers need to win another World Series soon."

"Thank God the Raiders fled to Oakland."

The Sixth Street exit drops you off right in the heart of Skid Row—Homeless Central, U.S.A., where in the afternoons the vets push shopping carts loaded with a lifetime full of found essentials, in the evenings dealers push their assorted cache of uppers, downers, and psychedelics to the slumming CPAs and college frat boys prepping for the weekend ahead, and at nights, the local heroin-addicted prostitutes turn tricks in converted port-a-potties that line the run-down boulevards in the shadow of the Sixth Street Bridge.

Travel ten minutes in any direction and you are in some of the prettiest areas Southern California can offer: the reinvigorated downtown, replete with the post-modern Disney Concert Hall, the stunning Our Lady of the Angels Cathedral, the timeless Museum of Contemporary Art; Beverly Hills, whose sprawling mansions house the actors most responsible for conscripting the mythology of the place, perhaps none more so than Bad Boy Drive, the famed just-beneath-the-clouds street whose three estates are inhabited by Jack Nicholson, Warren Beatty, and the corpulent, still-paying-off-his-palimony ghost of Marlon Brando, who, no matter how many Polynesian women he infected with the clap, no matter how many of his kids wound up in jail, still was a made man out here because of his barrier-busting performances in *A Streetcar Named Desire, On the Waterfront,* and *The Godfather.* They say Hollywood is an unforgiving place, but it really isn't true. Make one great movie and you're a star, make two great movies and you're a legend, make three great movies and you'll be a god until the end of time.

I drove past the old Angels Flight train-car tracks, a water-powered cable car that was a remnant from a vanished world, but which stubbornly held on, an electric Sisyphus forever pushing the downtown citizens up the hill which they would have to climb again the following day. I stopped off at a hamburger stand on the corner and had the best two cheeseburgers of my life before getting back into the car and driving the rest of the way to the fair.

By the time I reached the fairgrounds it was 5:30 in the evening. Game Three of the NBA Finals was about to start, the Lakers needing a victory against the hated Celtics to take a 2-1 advantage and I had the pregame show on, the announcers discussing what the Lakers needed to do to regroup from their poor showing in Game Two, when they had let Ray Allen, one of the league's deadliest perimeter shooters, kill them from behind the three-point line. It was the type of evening that made you feel lucky to be an Angeleno. Yes, the traffic was a nightmare, the air was giving you early emphysema, and the real estate was so expensive you had to rob a bank before considering the possibility of buying a home, but we had the Lakers, and when the Lakers were good, that nearly evened up the score.

As Janie had warned me, parking *was* an all-out nightmare. Steinbeck once wrote that someday "all the adolescents in the entire world will wind up in Los Angeles," but the truth is that at rush hour on a Thursday night it felt like they had already arrived, and that, should you drive to the city limits, you could, if you had the good fortune to be traveling on a day when there was little smog, look clean

31

across the rest of the world and see it had become one vast ghost town: Paris and London and Prague and Melbourne and Baghdad and Tehran and Tel Aviv, all of them deserted, empty sets in a long-ago completed film, quiet as a thousand sphinxes, their citizens all gone across the ocean to the Land of Milk and Honey.

It took another thirty minutes to find a parking spot, and then fifteen more to trek to the fairgrounds' entrance. Considering how difficult it had been to get to the fairgrounds, I suspected this would be the first and last time they held it downtown. Truth be told, I could have taken a cab from where I parked and found the fare worth paying, so by the time I walked up to the gate to buy my ticket it was nearly 7pm. A little breeze rolled across the makeshift rooftops of the carnival booths, the big-top tents and rising roller coasters turning back the clock to 1935, children chomping down on cotton candy and their parents pushing strollers across the crowded sprawl of circus games and gypsy dens.

There he was, his hair gone gray, tattoos crawling up his neck, in weathered black jeans and leather work boots, a silver bracelet and a mustache that had not been seen since the 1970s heyday of Van Nuys pornographic films. Crazy Dave Grushecky was inching towards old age, but he was clearly still a killer, and the way he leaned against the wall beside the corndog stand let anyone who might have been looking for a fight know that they should look elsewhere for a challenger.

Two other men stood with him, the three of them talking calmly, as if they were deciding which biker bar to hit after the fair was closed, or perhaps discussing whether the pretty forty-something woman who was working the chocolate malt machine would give any one of them the time of day. I waited until the two men walked away, moving in the direction of the restrooms, before I approached.

He saw me before I reached him, smiled broadly, and walked towards me with his right hand outstretched.

"Jesus, kid. You didn't even need to call. I'd recognize you anywhere."

He paused.

"Janie called a few minutes after you did. I'm sorry. Hassan was a good man and a great friend."

"Yeah, they don't make them like him anymore," I said.

"They never did, kid. They never did."

And then, before I had a chance to say *why* I had wanted to see him, Dave shook my hand a second time, pulled me close, nodded back in the direction of the tent just twenty feet away, that proclaimed COME SEE THE LARGEST HORSE IN NORTH AMERICA, TWO DOLLARS, smiled, and said:

"We're going to steal that horse tonight."

And as he started to walk away, he turned and said:

"About your father's medal," Dave said.

I nodded.

"I'll tell you everything you need to know. Let's just break this stallion out of jail first, eh? Meet you back here at 10pm."

He had brought Janie to the fair the night before because she liked to drive the go-carts, and she had a sweet tooth for the deep fried Snickers that they didn't sell in stores.

33

"Besides," he'd added, "any time you can win your girl a giant stuffed panda bear, that's an opportunity you don't pass up." They had wandered into the horse exhibit because, he said, he had ridden since he was a little boy, and because he wanted to see if there could really be some truth in advertising anywhere within the Los Angeles city limits.

It *was* true. The horse, his coat a muddy white, his legs long enough to be telephone poles, according to Dave, was enormous, a Sasquatch of a stallion, the kind of creature Zeus would have been riding had he ever come to Venice Beach to lift some weights. But what struck Dave more than the horse's size was the sight of a bunch of drunken revelers scaring the horse with their catcalls and mean-spirited taunts to such an extent that the horse spent the entire night standing in the farthest corner of the stable, his head turned to the curtain of the tent, a giant trying to hide his massive frame from the gawking eyes of the very worst Southern California had to offer.

Though Janie immediately walked out of the tent, her eyes beginning to mist up, Dave had already started making plans for how to liberate the stallion from his current plight. Or, as he put it, "it was my turn to play Moses." Dave knew of two honest men who knew how to steal and not get caught who could help him pull off the job. But the sudden presence of an able fourth was a blessing he was not about to turn away.

"There's a reason for everything in this world, kid," he told me. "And the reason you showed up here tonight was to help us steal that regal creature."

For the next ten minutes I tried to get my head around what Dave and his buddies were planning to do. After thinking it through, I worked up some rather grandiose and high-level expectation that our horse stealing would be the L.A. Fair version of the triple hotel heist in the George Clooney-led remake of *Ocean's 11*, something with so much élan and panache that you couldn't help but embrace it, even though it was illegal. But moments later I learned that Dave was rather more old-fashioned in his planning:

"Okay, here's what we're gonna do: we hide beneath the petting zoo bleachers until the place closes, we bust the lock on the horse's stable with a crowbar, and then we put him in the trailer of John's truck. Piece of cake."

We were a long way from Danny Ocean on this one.

Just after Dave got me up to speed on the "nuances" of the heist, he introduced me to the aforementioned John (who went 6'-6" and at least 275, like a taller Joe Frazier) and Pete (who was shorter, six feet tops, but who still clocked in at somewhere in the neighborhood of 225, and who looked like Babe Ruth's older brother). The three of them had first met back in the early 1980s, when they were doing freelance deep-sea welding off the coast of Key West.

They had stayed in touch through the years, all three of them probably the oddest-looking Greenpeace activists anyone had ever seen—the trio dressed like ex-bikers who had happily settled into a second life as extras in old 1980s cop movies, the types that usually starred a pair of ethnically and behaviorally mismatched partners who drove cars way above their pay grade and somehow always had enough bullets in their chambers to kill forty-seven men without reloading.

The bleachers did not provide the cover that big men like Pete and John required, so we instead walked into the livestock stables that were closed to the public, discreetly moving through a door marked No Admittance and then slipping beneath a set of wooden gateways that led to the pens. These were the contest animals who would not be on display until later in the week, among them twenty or thirty pigs, fifteen or twenty goats, a handful of llamas, and about thirty sheep so tightly packed into a small space that you could not see the ground beneath them.

"They'll never find us here," Dave said.

If there was one moment's hesitation that I might have been rash in my decision to suddenly agree to join this band of merry thieves, it was then, climbing over the holding fence and sitting down in a corner of the pen, surrounded by admittedly gentle animals for whom we have so much to be thankful for, yet whose overwhelming foul odors immediately had me breathing into the collar of my shirt.

"Don't worry, kid," Slim Pete said as he slid down next to me. "Only fifteen minutes to closing time. A couple of hours from now we'll all be drinking Heinekens out in the San Gabriel Mountains."

We spent the next hour doing what guys do best: shooting the shit. We spoke of sports (we all agreed Kobe Bryant was as good as Michael Jordan, Pete going so far as to say that he was even better), music (The Temptations over The Supremes, The Four Tops over both of them), movies (Pacino over De Niro, Newman over Brando), women (in her prime, Elizabeth Taylor was the most beautiful woman of the twentieth century), literature (*The Grapes of Wrath* was the Great American Novel), travel (London was overrated), cars (the BMW Roadster was a thing of beauty), and religion (hell yeah God existed).

We spoke about politics:

"The greatest presidents of the twentieth century were all philanderers," Slim Pete said.

"Get out of here," Dave answered, waving him off.

"Think about it," Pete insisted. "Eisenhower had Kay Sommersby, J.F.K. had Marilyn Monroe and Judith Exner, not to mention every hooker between Hyannis Port and D.C. L.B.J. had all those Texas belles, Clinton had Gennifer Flowers and Monica Lewinsky. Heck, F.D.R. was in a wheelchair and he was still scoring major trim."

"The man's got a point," John responded, shaking his head. "The man's got one hell of a point."

"Meanwhile all the God-fearing, self-righteous pols— Woodrow Wilson, Dick Nixon, Jimmy Carter, George W.— were utter failures. Had those guys chased a little more pussy we all would have been better off," Pete said.

"But don't you think less of them knowing they were screwing around?" Dave asked. Though he'd deny it if anyone ever said it, it took me all of twenty minutes in his company to see Dave was a romantic at heart, and that Janie was the love of his life.

"Heck no," Pete answered.

"A man's right to cheat is based upon how much good he does for others," Pete continued. "J.F.K. had every right to wander because he wrote the Civil Rights Bill, saved us from WWIII with Castro and the Russians, and was probably the single most important American of the twentieth century. He earned his play. But Tiger Woods? Please. Guy treats people like garbage his entire career, refuses to sign autographs for kids, never takes a stand on social issues, and swears like a sailor up and down the golf course. You're going to be a jerk like that, you'd better keep it in your pants."

By this point all of us were trying not to laugh, and we slid further down into the corner of the pen and hoped the braying sounds of feeding sheep were drowning out our conversation.

To be inside the fairgrounds after hours is a magical, melancholy experience. With the game booths boarded up for the night, the painted clowns and mermaids and soaring superheroes subdued in silhouette, the ice cream carts dead-bolted with combination locks like little mobile safes, the rides that, only hours earlier, ferried groups of children into the sky, sound-tracked by organ, glockenspiel and banjos straight out of an otherwise long-vanished America, and the Ferris wheel, constant as a neon North Star, compass for every tourist driver lost somewhere within a ten mile radius, you feel as if you have stepped outside of time completely and somehow landed in an otherworld that has been created by a god who grew up reading Lewis Carroll's *Alice in Wonderland* and listening to Syd Barrett-era Pink Floyd.

Contrary to popular belief, the truth about county fairs is that most carnies are flush enough with money to be able to outsource much of their payroll. High school kids on summer vacation man the various booths and rides, while the carnies themselves usually shack up at local motels rather than stay in the sleeping compartments of the trailers and big-rigs they have driven to their most recent multi-week destination. Because of this, there aren't more than a handful of people awake on the grounds in the middle of the night, and most of them are security guards, really just kids from

L.A. City College and Cal State L.A. wearing company-issued yellow jackets and taking advantage of the darkness to smoke pot in one of the only quiet places in greater Los Angeles.

I learned all of this from Pete, who, in addition to having an impressively developed—and equally offbeat—opinion when it came to male sexual behavior, was apparently a gifted recon man.

"I learned it in Vietnam," he said. "Only skill I ever picked up in the military."

"Well Pete," Dave responded. "It sure is paying off tonight."

During the process of his recon, Pete had learned that the two security guys in "Zone D" were two first-class druggies. "Call 'em Mutt and Jeff. Rosencrantz and Guildenstern. Whatever you like. Two stoners with a sweet tooth who don't even do their rounds. They just sit underneath the back awning of the wild western nerf gun range, smokin' out and eatin' twinkies."

"They'll be a quarter of a mile away from Big Chief," Pete added.

"That's good work, Pete," John said, taking another swig of Pepsi.

Things went wrong from the start. John tripped over a stray electric cable that was charged with keeping the LOST IN THE FUNHOUSE sign blazing neon all night, which resulted in a cut lip, a chipped tooth, and a sudden power outage that left us, literally, stumbling through the dark. A few moments later Pete realized he had left the bolt cutters back in the petting zoo pen, which meant we all stood in the shadows for a solid five minutes while Pete doubled-back to retrieve them.

He returned, naturally, empty-handed.

"Where are they?" Dave asked, concern beginning to creep into his voice.

"I don't know. It's like the Bermuda Triangle of Straw back there," Pete answered, with the slow, I-can't-believe-it-drawl of a man who has just seen Bigfoot thumbing a ride out on Interstate 5 deep in the Oregon wilds.   "What are we going to do now?" John asked.

"Let's just get to that damned stable," Dave said.

It was as if Dave was aware the circumstances had nearly caused him to retreat, and, in disbelief and horror that it had—however fleetingly—occurred to him to raise the white flag, he now was doubling-down on the gamble he had already put into motion.

"I hate county fairs," he added. "Absolutely hate 'em."

I should not have been surprised at such hiccups, of course. I'd seen enough crime movies to know this stuff never went as planned. In *Bonnie and Clyde*, C.W. Moss parallel parks the getaway car into such a tight spot that the crew almost doesn't make it out of their first bank heist alive; in *Heat*, Robert De Niro's crew is done in by a random tip-off that somehow reaches cop Al Pacino's desk minutes before the job goes down.

The next surprise came when we got to the stable, only to see that the formerly padlocked gate was cracked open a good six inches, and the oversized combination lock left lying on the ground at Dave's feet.

And we could hear voices coming from inside the stable.

We crept in slowly, like a crouching conga line without the music. Somehow I had wound up second in formation, behind only Dave, our de facto leader, the small-time, county fair equivalent of Lieutenant Kilgore in *Apocalypse Now*, the V.C.-baiting wild man who would let nothing—not mortar fire, not napalm—stop him from surfing the beaches along the coasts of Vietnam.

There they were. Laurel and Hardy. They were trying to lasso the horse, their yellow security jackets removed in order to display their matching black t-shirts, which had the following acronym emblazoned in bright yellow letters across their backs: PETA.

"YOU HAVE GOT TO BE KIDDING ME!" Dave shouted.

I put my hand on his shoulder in a hopeless attempt to get him to calm down.

"Jesus," Pete whispered behind me. "You'd think they were the ATF or the DEA with those shirts."

"For a minute I thought we'd walked in on a drug bust," he added.

The two activists dropped their respective holds on the lasso, the stallion immediately retreating to the furthest corner of the stable. It was clear by the look on the poor creature's face that he was thinking something along the lines of, "with friends like these…"

After a few seconds' pause, however, it was clear we had walked into the horse-stealing version of the O.K. Corral, six would-be rustlers, unequally divided, staring one another down, cigarettes and brownies in our pockets instead of firearms.

Laurel spoke first:

"Who the hell are you guys?"

"We've come to liberate this horse," John said, his voice shaking the sides of the tent as if he were an old Puritan preacher in one of the founding churches, reminding everyone in attendance that they were all sinners in the hands of an angry God, and eternal damnation would be theirs.

"Yeah, well, we were here first," Hardy said, breathlessly. The failed lasso attempt had winded him.

"Look, kids. Why don't you guys go back to putting up crazy freeway billboards that turn even decent people against your cause, and leave this to us?" Dave asked.

"This whole country probably would have gone cage-free twenty years ago if not for the kind of bush-league stunts you pull," Pete added.

"Listen, old man," Hardy replied. "We've been working security for two straight weeks planning this break, and we're not about to let some trigger-happy veterans still fighting the Vietnam War step in and screw it up for us."

Dave pulled the gun so fast that Billy the Kid himself would have been impressed.

"Well, there is one thing all of us can agree on," Dave warned. "That horse's life is worth more than any man's here."

With the unexpected realization that someone might actually get shot over this—STAND-OFF IN HORSE PEN AT L.A. FAIR ENDS IN GUNFIGHT. TWO HIPPIES WHO DIDN'T REALIZE THE 1960S WERE OVER,

DEAD—I stepped in front of Dave, and turned my body so I could see both Dave and the PETA twins.

I reached toward Dave's gun, and lightly touched my fingers to the gun. There was moisture on the barrel.

"Put down the gun, man. Look," I said, then turned to stare at Laurel and Hardy, the lasso now lying on the sawdust like casually discarded laundry. "Where were you guys planning on taking him?"

They shifted their feet, looked at one another, then back at me, then down at the ground again.

"We," Hardy began—he had become the unofficial spokesman for the two of them—"there's a…Well, we figured we'd make a few calls once we got on the road."

"Two weeks planning and that's what they come up with!" Dave shouted.

By this point, Big Chief had lain down in the straw, his eyes closed, clearly disinterested in the showdown that was unfolding in his stable.

I was getting tired.

"Hey Guys," I said, "We're all on the same side here. This horse deserves better. The guys who own him don't deserve the honor, and the people who come to gawk at him deserve to be lined up and shot for such cruel inhumanity."

"But it's almost midnight," I continued, aware I was starting to sound like a second-rate send-up of Churchill, all forced poetry and pomposity, "and if we're going to get this horse out of here, we need to do it now."

I looked between the guys, Laurel and Hardy shuffling their feet in the straw, Dave trying to hide the fact his pistol—clearly a prop he'd stolen from one of the water-shooting ranges over near the rollercoaster—was leaking, and

Pete and John both still poised to rush their enemies and win the war their country had not allowed them to win nearly forty years ago.

"I tell you what," I said. "You two can take the credit for the theft. PETA could use some good publicity, what with the psychotic things you guys usually get yourselves into."

"Hey—" Hardy tried to interject.

"Don't fight it. It's true," I said. "You guys take credit for the heist, and you can help us load him in the trailer and drive with us out to the ranch that these guys have lined up. From what I hear it's gorgeous," I lied, having heard nothing at all about where we were taking him. "Big Chief will have so many acres and pastures to graze in and run through it will be like the Wild West all over again. And you'd better take it. Otherwise I'm going to let him shoot you with that water gun of his he's packing."

"Damnit," Dave said, throwing his hands in the air, Pete and John both laughing openly.

After another moment or two, agreement was signaled by the fact that everyone simply shrugged their shoulders and climbed the little wooden fence into the stable, talking softly to the horse that had opened up its eyes in recognition that an accord had been reached.

I felt like Nelson Mandela, and wondered if all great peace agreements were arrived at when both parties had simply tired of the struggle, that it was not man's better angels shining through, but the more modest and quite understandable fact that everyone just wanted to go home and get some sleep. Either way, the rest of the heist went smoothly. The horse was an active and enthusiastic participant in his own escape, and our makeshift, impromptu, illegal caravan was on the freeway by 1am.

By 2am we were sitting on the porch steps of a ranch high up in the San Gabriel mountains, looking onto verdant prairies, a handful of little creeks, and enough starlight to enable you to read a book until the sun returned come morning.

"Wow," I said to Dave as we looked out onto the sprawling landscape. "Are we still in Southern California?"

"It's one of the last great secrets of this area," he said, his voice barely above a whisper, as if in deference to the goats that slept like dreaming silhouettes all across the field that we looked out onto.

We sat in silence for a little while, watching as Big Chief slowly trotted across the tall grass of his new home with the air of a kid who had not expected so many gifts beneath the tree on Christmas, and so who circles the house's bottom floor in a marveled daze for an hour before he regains his bearings and settles on a toy to play with.

"As for the medal," Dave began, his face glowing in the light of an enormous moon, the horse now gone into a breakneck sprint out across the fields, disappearing into the patch of trees at the far edge of our sightline.

"There's a man up north. A priest your father was good friends with. Used to teach at the University, though he may be retired by now. Look him up when you get there."

Chapter 2
Return to the Land of the Flower Children

My parents met in San Francisco. It was 1973. Willie Mays had headed east the previous year, doomed to end his marvelous career stumbling out in centerfield playing for the New York Mets, and the former stars that had helped Mays turn the Giants into perennial contenders—the fearless, high-kicking pitcher Juan Marichal and the long-ball hitting right-fielder Willie McCovey—were both entering the twilights of their respective careers. The Zodiac Killer was on the loose, a faceless Grendel haunting every part of the city, and the Summer of Love had years earlier turned into one long, increasingly paranoid nightmare of an acid trip, as the hippies and the holdouts, the wounded veterans and the failed rock stars all downshifted from the free-love ethos of the 1960s to an often homicidal despair by the time that Richard Nixon won his reelection. My parents lived off campus at the intersection of Haight and Stanyon, just across the street from a Golden Gate Park far removed from the one that hosted blissed-out drum circles only four or five summers prior. My parents' San Francisco was a dark place: it had more in common with the foggy London streets of Conan Doyle's Sherlock Holmes than it did the spirited utopia that Kesey's Band of Merry Pranksters had wanted it to be. The San Francisco of my mother and father was ground zero of the decade after, one long hangover in the Age of Watergate and Ho Chi Minh. In her letters of the time, my mother writes unceasingly of union strikes, off-campus assaults, and enough veterans' protests to make it seem that the city was on the verge of chaos. Indeed, the city that my father landed in when he first arrived from overseas was most likely not what he had expected, if he had expected anything at all. Instead of strummed guitars and women walking around North Beach with flowers in their hair, there were chalk outlines on the sidewalks and the National Guard patrolling the steps of City Hall in the wake of yet another violent protest.

But I loved the city. I went there at least twice a year, eating in the same diners my parents used to take me to, riding the cable cars from Ghirardelli Square to Fisherman's Wharf just as my parents had on their very first date, the night my mother said that my father, immigrant poor—"he landed with a jacket, a suitcase, and an encyclopedic knowledge of the fights of Muhammad Ali"—gave away his coat to a corner busker who had just played a lovely version of The Beatles' "I'll Follow the Sun," a song my father didn't understand by a band that he had never heard of. I knew I was romanticizing, and that to visit San Francisco with money in your pocket was much different than to try to live there when you did not know where your next meal was going to come from, but the truth was that I knew this was where my parents had met and fallen in love, where both of their lives had been changed forever, and where I knew that they had been happiest. That meant an enormous amount to me.

The name Crazy Dave had mentioned to me was one I remembered hearing in my parents' conversations, a voice I had come across once or twice on the telephone when I answered it while my parents were in another room, a good-natured Irish brogue that would ask, "Sonny, is your father there?" What I most remembered about that voice was that I was certain it was coming from a place where an eternal rainbow was involved, where little smiling men sat upon steel buckets filled with lavish treasure, where winged fairies fluttered through the skies and sang the types of songs my mother used to sing to me when I had trouble sleeping.

The back-story:

Father Jim O'Leary was the man who found my father sleeping on a bench in Golden Gate Park. My father had arrived two weeks before the fall semester began, and a full week before his scholarship was to begin, and he did not have the money to both afford a meal once a day and a roof above his head each night. "Food will always win," he told me once, when I asked my father which he chose. Father Jim had secured him a room in an SRO near Howard Street, and gave him enough money for three meals a day to last him through the week.

"And buy yourself some boots, son," Jim had told my father. "Those sneakers won't last a week in this weather."

I don't think I had ever met Father Jim O'Leary face to face, but his presence was yet another welcome ghost in an apartment that was full of them—proof that there were components of the Church still worth being proud of, and, more importantly, proof that America was a place where a middle-eastern college student could be made to feel the world was his, if indeed he wanted it to be.

"I don't know if he's still alive," Dave had said, as the two of us had sat upon the porch steps. "But if he is, he's still in San Francisco. He wasn't built for anywhere else on Earth. Oh, and kid," Dave added, as he started to rise, his adrenaline high beginning to subside in the wake of our wild theft, "Fly into Oakland. San Francisco International is for tourists and yuppies."

If Jim O' Leary was still practicing, he would be at the church on the campus of the University where my mother went to mass all those years ago: St. Ignatius, whose façade was just a few blocks from Golden Gate Park and the Haight-Ashbury intersection where so many psychedelic rock bands got their fabled starts.

I checked into the Palace Hotel, made legendary by the fact that Enrico Caruso, the greatest of Italian opera singers, was staying at the hotel in 1906 when the city went up in flames as a result of a catastrophic earthquake. In 1989, during the city's second major earthquake of the century, I was staying with my parents in the Palace, as we were minutes away from attending Game One of the 1989 Subway Series between the Giants and the Oakland A's. Unlike Caruso, who swore never to return to the city, I stayed in the Palace every time I came to visit. Not only did it remind me of my parents, but I felt like the hotel was a touchstone for me, proof that I had lived through a mythic moment in modern American history.

I woke early, took a swim in the hotel's swimming pool, showered, dressed in a pair of grey woolen slacks, a black button-up shirt and a pair of black boots, and took the elevator down to the lobby. I purchased half an hour of computer time from the front desk, and did a Google search for Father Jim O'Leary.

There was no record of him teaching at the university: he wasn't listed as the instructor of record for any courses, nor did his name appear anywhere on the St. Ignatius Cathedral's web page. Dave was right: the man was either retired or dead, and even though Google's main page did return a few scattered entries on Father Jim O'Leary's career—the two books of spiritualist poetry he had published back in the mid-1970s, the second one earning him the esteemed PEN Award—it was again clear that Jim was not a man who had accepted technology into his purified heart. If I was going to find him—as had been the case with Dave Grushecky—I was going to have to do it the old-fashioned way.

After the assorted telephone numbers associated with the rectory and the Religious Studies Department went unanswered, I figured the best place to start would be to ask around on campus and see if anyone had any sense of where Jim, if he was still alive, might be living, or even better, perhaps had a contact number or forwarding address where I could reach him.

I left the hotel and stepped out onto New Montgomery Street. It was packed with cars, taxis ferrying tourists from one local attraction to another, luxury cars taking accountants and tax attorneys who had lunched at the Top of the Mark or John's Steak House back to their offices in the heart of the financial district, and ramshackle vans driven by aging hippies now living off of Social Security checks and their hazy memories of the Summer of Love, their tie-dyed t-shirts and MAKE LOVE NOT WAR bumper stickers seeming more sadly futile than optimistically buoyant.

"Why the traffic?" I asked the doorman, a middle-aged African-American who looked like he had once played outside linebacker for the 49ers.

"Protests down in Golden Gate Park and across the rest of the city today," he said, his voice struggling to survive above the din of horns and music sidling out of open car windows.

"Who's protesting?"

"Half the damned city," he answered. "The Get Out of Afghanistan Crew. The usual shit: "Give Them Back Their Oil," "American Satan." He started to laugh, shaking his head.

"It's San Francisco, man. We always need a Vietnam, you know? Bring back the Jefferson Airplane and all that LSD. This place is like a broken-hearted ex-girlfriend: it never moves on."

We shared a laugh, he tipped his hat goodbye. I walked down New Montgomery in the direction of the BART station. I would avoid the traffic by traveling underground.

Inside there were the usual city hipsters, twenty-something men with three-day beards, Converse high tops, skinny denim jeans and flannel shirts from vintage Berkeley stores, girls in knee-length skirts with nose rings, purple lipstick, and skater boots; there was an Asian man who looked as old as God himself playing far-eastern folk songs on a beat-up zither that sounded lovely over the rumble of the subway cars, there were Oakland heavies in Raiders hats and sagging jeans, checking their cell phones for the latest news on their beloved Golden State Warriors. To get a feel for a city there is nothing like the subway: it's the kind of democratic space where people who would otherwise never cross each other's paths come together to make sure everyone arrives at their destinations safely.

I took a seat at the back of the car, across from a beauty in her early thirties dressed in a linen suit, her eyes glued to a paperback copy of *Leaves of Grass*.

I closed my eyes and tried to sleep. It felt like I hadn't slept in days. I didn't dream.

When I woke I felt like Harrison Ford in the early scenes of *Blade Runner*: a man living in a futuristic landscape that he recognized as his own and yet could not believe had come to pass. The subway train ran through tunnels like those flying cars that Ford's Lt. Deckard piloted through a post-apocalyptic Los Angeles, and for a moment I imagined the passengers that surrounded me were the real-life versions of the Replicants Deckard has been assigned to track. As the newspaper that the man who sat in the aisle across from me was reading stated in bold black letters, we were living in the AGE OF THE CLONE, and the truth was that anything we could imagine might someday be invented had probably already hit the streets. But today I wasn't tracking high-end automatons, technologically advanced machines wrapped in flesh and blood. I was searching for a priest in an enormous city who might have died several years ago.

I exited the BART station. The streets were eerily empty for such a lovely Saturday afternoon. In fact, they looked as if they had been evacuated, and the silence allowed me to hear the far-off shouts and sirens and music that I knew was at the center of the protest. I should have known. Injustice called the people of this city to gather where their voices would best be heard; and there was nowhere better to be heard in all the city than within its tended Eden, Golden Gate Park.

I decided to bypass the protest by avoiding the park entirely. Instead, I walked out of my way for several blocks and then circled back towards the campus, and as I did so I thought about how Golden Gate Park had been the site of one of the most special, and unexpected, moments of my life.

It was ten summers prior that I had met Bob Dylan in Golden Gate Park. He was sitting on a park bench eating a sandwich as I came down the path with an ex-girlfriend's dog as my companion. When I sat down next to him, he nodded, and I nodded back, and that was it. The two of us sat there, watching a group of kids play soccer in a little clearing about twenty yards from us, and after about ten minutes or so the dog, an old golden retriever who would meet his maker six months later after a short bout with cancer, got restless, and as I rose to leave, I turned to him and said,

"Thank you for all of the wonderful music."

He nodded again, and I walked away. I never told the story to anyone because I always worried it would have cheapened the experience—it was like going out for a casual stroll and happening to meet Jesus Christ when you stopped to take a rest, except that Jesus never wrote "Mr. Tambourine Man"—and that, since there wasn't exactly a conversation, people wouldn't have understood why it was such a big deal to me.

Though there was the constant, inaudible hum of cheering, chanting, singing voices from down in the Park—as if I were a man walking by a jam-packed baseball stadium on the day of an afternoon doubleheader—the lovely homes all along the boulevards were as quiet as they always were: sentinels as silent as the British guards stationed before the gates of Buckingham Palace, impervious to noise and menace. At the end of the block there was a liquor store with a poster tacked to its front window announcing the imminent arrival of U2, the greatest of Irish bands who had come the closest to approaching the cultural dominance and melodic beauty of The Beatles. Figuring I was going to be doing some serious walking for the rest of the afternoon, I headed inside to purchase a bottle of water. It was like a general store in a newly created ghost town: the counterman asleep, the television above his head showing the highlights of last night's NBA playoff games, Steve Nash whirling through traffic before throwing a perfectly-timed behind-the-back pass to a streaking Vince Carter for an easy lay-up, followed by Dwayne Wade jamming home a thundering slam dunk in fast-break transition. As I walked back to the glass refrigerators at the southern end of the store, I noticed a young girl, ten or eleven years old, her eyes fixed on the multi-colored lines of soda-cans shining underneath the lights like mannequins in a department store window. I knew that look: it was the look that all young kids have when there are no parents around to tell them what they could and couldn't buy, and more importantly, what they could and couldn't drink. It was no surprise that five seconds later she pulled down a two-liter bottle of Dr. Pepper from the shelf and began to walk happily back down the aisle. I settled for a bottle of Evian water.

The store was as quiet as a church, and the clerk, God bless him, had actually begun to snore. The girl and I looked at each other, both of us trying not to laugh too loudly. She shrugged her shoulders and asked, "Should we wake him up?"

"I'd feel bad doing that. I haven't slept that well in years," I said. "Let's just leave the money on the counter."

As the girl fumbled around in her purple backpack, its canvas material covered in stickers of rock and roll bands from several generations back, I pulled a five dollar bill out of my wallet and said quietly, "It's on me, kid."

"Thanks," she said, offering a good-natured salute as she headed for the door.

On the sidewalk the girl was squinting into the light, looking as if she was waiting for a ride, or, though far less likely, for a supernatural sign to let her know what she should do next.

"You okay, kid?" I asked. "Someone coming to pick you up?"

Being the smart, street savvy city girl that I was glad to see that she was, she hesitated, looked at me and nodded.

"I'm meeting my sister down the block."

"Good. Take care of yourself," I said, and started walking in the opposite direction, up towards the cathedral that was a few blocks up and a few more over.

I had walked maybe thirty feet before I heard the girl say,

"Any chance I can borrow five dollars for the BART?"

I turned and began to walk back towards her, saying as I walked, "What about your sister?"

"Well," she began, trying to sustain the confidence and independence she had first displayed when we left the store. "We were down at the protests. It was pretty crazy. We got separated. I'd call her, but I don't have a cell phone. And neither does she."

"How old are you?" I asked.

"Eleven."

I had just come from the BART station. It was a good fifteen-minute walk through some rather isolated areas.

Damnit, I thought to myself. If it's not a horse that needs to be stolen, it's a kid who's too young to travel alone. Somewhere my father's ghost was laughing, I knew. *This is what happens when you're raised by a mother as good as yours was*, I could hear him saying. *Conscience will get you every time.*

At this rate it'd be the middle of next year by the time I found the medal. My father would have been dead long enough to have made it to Heaven, found out it wasn't all that he thought it would be, and talked his guardian angel into finding him a new body to inhabit on Earth, a la Warren Beatty in *Heaven Can Wait*.

"I tell you what, kid. Let's share a cab. I don't want you walking too far on your own. This isn't the greatest area."

"You don't have to do that, Mister," she said, her girlish swagger returning. "I know the city like the back of my hand. The BART's just a little way's east," she said, pointing due south.

"East is that way, kid," I nodded. "Your parents taught you never to talk to strangers, right?"

She nodded, squinting again from the light of the sun.

"Well, I'm Patrick," I said, extending my hand.

"Dorothy," she said. We shook hands.

"Ok, good," I said. "Now I'm not a stranger."

"Actually, they say most people are killed by people they know," Dorothy said. "So I was probably safer when I didn't know your name."

The kid was funny enough to make me wonder if her sister hadn't simply ditched her in frustration at the girl's sharp wit, but I kept those thoughts to myself.

"Well, it's too late now," I said. "You'll just have to take your chances. Come on," I said, starting to cross the street that ran parallel to the park below. "You can tell me how you and your sister got separated while we're on the lookout for a cab."

As we began to walk through the quiet streets, it became immediately clear that Dorothy was a first-class motor-mouth, a one-girl wrecking ball of narrative and opinion.

"We were down there," she said, pointing in the direction of the park. "We were with some of her friends. I got separated from everyone when the band came onstage. I couldn't see anything. I thought if I came up the hill I might be able to pick her out. But there are too many people down there. You'd think it was the March on Washington, or that The Beatles had gotten back together. Anyway, this happens all the time with Gemma—her name's Gemma, but my mom used to call her Marian, because she likes old movies and Robin Hood is her favorite and Maid Marian is the love of his life and she helps him steal all that money from the rich and give it to the poor which my sister thinks is how America should be—anyway, this happens all the time with Gemma. I love her but she's a space cadet, always forgetting to pay our electricity bill, losing her keys more often than most people wash their hands, falling in love with guys who even *I* know are bad news."

As the monologue progressed, she started to sound like a narrator in a Faulkner story, or a baseball announcer, Vin Scully perhaps, stringing together words and phrases in such a way that her long sentences began to approach a kind of poetry. Stranded in the city of Kerouac and Ginsberg, she was a resurrected Beat, a child bopper teasing out her inner Di Prima.

Of all the liquor stores in all the world, I joked to myself, *the eleven-year-old play-by-play announcer had to walk into mine.*

"…There was a rumor her favorite band was going to make a surprise appearance today. You know The Grateful Dead? Their lead singer, Jerry Garcia, looked like Santa Claus, although if he was, his bag of presents would have been filled with ecstasy and LSD and marijuana and PCP, you know? 'Twas the Night Before Christmas, Tune in, Turn On, Tune Out, Noel, Noel…Well, he's dead. Eight or nine years now, I think. Maybe longer. But the rest of the guys are still alive, and they live around here, at least some of them do, and Gemma wanted to see them, and she thought I should see them, since she's been playing their records for me nonstop since I was a baby."

She looked up at me. She seemed to be in the process of deciding whether she should continue. Surprisingly, she decided to wind down her monologue for a minute to ask a question.

"You like them?"

"Who? The Grateful Dead?" I asked, surprised. "Yeah, sure. They jam a little too much for my taste though. Those guitar solos go on forever."

She laughed. Okay, the kid had thrown a wrench into my day but at least she had a sense of humor. I was liking her more and more by the minute.

She asked another question.

"What kind of music do you like, then?"

"Springsteen. Petty. Lennon. McCartney. Dylan. Prince. Seger. Neil Young. Stevie Wonder."

"I like The-Artist-Formerly-Known-As-I'm-A-Guitar-God-Who-Also Likes-To-Cross-Dress too," she said. "He's a genius."

I had spent the majority of my adult life relatively sure I didn't want to have children. Much of that was because I had been so focused professionally that I worried that raising a child would permanently push me off track, swallowing the time that I wanted to write and paint. Although, if I was really honest with myself, a lot of it had even more to do with the fact that I was almost pathologically afraid of marriage, considering I was certain I didn't know anyone who was, or had ever been, happily married. But of course, as my father liked to say, "No one thinks they want kids until they spend five minutes with one. Then you realize that kids are a hell of a lot more fun than ninety-nine percent of the adults you're ever going to meet. And besides," he'd added. "You're a man. Picasso was in his 70s and he was still knocking up his models. You've got plenty of time."

When I came out of this momentary aside Dorothy had picked up another head of steam.

"...Anyway. The Dead never showed up. But the police did. And the Hell's Angels. Everyone says we should build a wall to keep the Latinos from crossing the border. But I say the wall we *need* to build is around every one of those Harley Dealerships. They've been messing things up since Altamont."

She was a pop culture savant, a Rain Man of pop radio, way too young to know as much as she did, way too articulate to be as young as she clearly was. Whatever the case, she was a good kid who I didn't want walking through the city alone. The search for Jim O'Leary was going to have to wait a few hours.

When Dorothy paused for breath I was surprised to realize I liked to listening to her mini orations. I figured another question would get her going again.

"Why doesn't your sister have a cell phone? Is she Amish?"

"No," Dorothy said. "She's not Amish. That would be entertaining though. She *did* play with the idea of being a Hari Krishna when she was like thirteen or so, but it fell through because she doesn't like airports. Anyway, Gemma doesn't...how can I say it? She doesn't believe in anything that's been invented after 1969. She's like one of those Intelligent Design believers, except her temple is the Fillmore West and her priest was, is, and will always be Ken Kesey. She's seen *Bonnie and Clyde* like five hundred times, but I don't think she's ever used a microwave oven. You probably think she's crazy," Dorothy said, looking up the street to where an old man pushed a shopping cart full of empty beer cans towards an intersection where the streetlights had malfunctioned.

"Well, she probably *is* crazy. Not in a bad way. And not in any way that makes it impossible for her to function. She knows how to drive. She has a good job. Well, a steady job at least. She dates guys and the occasional girl. She takes good care of me. It's just that she's nostalgic for an era that passed away long before she was ever even born. It doesn't really make sense to me. Except it sort of does, you know? I mean, she wishes she could have married Jerry Garcia, and I wish I could have won a fellowship to Hogwarts and been on the Quidditch team playing alongside Harry Potter. We all have our dreams."

She said this with such gravity that I made sure not to smile as she spoke, even though two things were clear: Dorothy was right about her sister being a space cadet, and Dorothy was fiercely, almost unimaginably smart. So smart, in fact, that I knew she would spend a lifetime surrounded by people who were either enchanted by or wholly intimidated by her intelligence. She would be loved often but rarely understood. My father would have identified with her dilemma.

We stopped at the corner, faced as we were with another light that was out of order. It was the second time that afternoon where I felt like I had wandered into a post-apocalyptic movie, an *I Am Legend* kind of feeling, where the hero is left to wander through deserted streets seeking food and water in a landscape that has suddenly been reduced to a chaotic mass of dilapidated structures and unpredictable weather patterns.

We walked on for a minute or so before I noticed Dorothy's cheeks were flushed and that she was clearly bothered by the sunlight.

"You wearing sunscreen, kid?" I asked.

"No. Gemma tells me there are chemicals in it that are worse for my skin than the sun."

"Well, what about baseball caps? Anything dangerous about those?"

"No. I don't think so," she said.

"All right, then. Keep a lookout for a mall or a sporting goods store. I don't want you getting so burned that you get heat stroke out here, okay?"

Chapter 3
Apartment Woodstock

Dorothy had told me she and Gemma lived in North Beach, the old Beatnik district that bordered Chinatown, and which boasted, in no particular order of importance, the famous City Lights Books, the infamous Condor Room strip club, a host of Italian restaurants, and St. Peter and Paul's Basilica, which was the cathedral where Joe DiMaggio and Marilyn Monroe had married. Though it was an old, crowded part of the city, where would-be artists and musicians eked out livings and homeless men slept on bus stop benches and in unkempt alleys, it still retained a magic that only a place like New York's Greenwich Village could equal. Indeed, it may not have been Paris in the 20s, but it did have a genuine bohemian sensibility that few other places still possessed. I made sure that we were walking in the general direction of North Beach while I kept scanning the intersections for signs of an available cab.

Dorothy told me the two of them had been living there for six months, since their mother had passed away— her second bout with breast cancer had simply been too much for her to fight—and Gemma had taken two jobs to keep the hot water running and the Amoeba Records purchases coming: in the afternoons she was a cashier at City Lights, and in the evenings she walked across the street to work the counter at the Beat Museum, a little two-story house of memorabilia that included paintings, letters, photographs, and out-of-print broadsides from the likes of Lawrence

Ferlinghetti, Allen Ginsberg, Jack Kerouac, Neil Cassady, Diane Di Prima and a printed cast of thousands. Dorothy, however, did not change schools, because she was on scholarship at The Sacred Heart School in Pacific Heights, one of the city's swankier sections.

"Gemma has a lot of friends," Dorothy said. "They're all a little weird, of course, but sweet. They have good hearts and we're never lonely and the boys are cute and the girls do my hair for me and let me hang around when they're listening to music and watching old movies and stuff."

I had found a black Giants cap in a CVS pharmacy, and I gave Dorothy the short spiel about the code that went with wearing such a cap: "This is the hat that Willie Mays wore. Wear it with integrity, honor, and a sense of justice. Got it?" I asked, mock seriously.

"Got it," she said enthusiastically. We started walking again.

"So Patrick," Dorothy said, sounding as if she was about to begin a little friendly interrogation of her own. "I don't think you ever said what you were doing in San Francisco."

"My father died last week. He was living in Iran. You know where that is?"

She nodded.

"You're a smart one, kiddo. Anyway, he was a great soccer player back in his day. Played for the National Team. Helped them win a Silver Medal in the World Championships back in the early '70s. It turns out he didn't take the medal with him when he moved back to Iran ten years ago. I don't know why. So I got a letter he had written asking that I retrieve the medal and have it interred with him back home."

"And it's in San Francisco?"

We stopped at an intersection. There were two young men holding hands beside us, one wearing dark eyeliner that gave him a mystical look, as if he were an ancient dervish or a lead singer in a British New Wave band from the years of Margaret Thatcher.

"It might be. A friend of my father's said it might be up here with another old friend of his."

We were on a boulevard lined with clothing shops, a flower store, and an old boutique that specialized in hand-made tapestries.

"You would have liked my father. He loved this city as much as your sister does. He always talked about how some of the best years of his life were spent here."

A few moments later a cab pulled up at a red light about twenty feet ahead of us, and we ran to catch up to it before the light changed.

"Eureka!" Dorothy joyously screamed as the car idled at the curb.

On the ride to North Beach, Dorothy peppered me with more questions about my father:

"How tall was he?"

"5'10."

"How much did he weigh?"

"Depends."

"On what?"

"On whether we are talking about his thirties or his forties."

She thought for a second.

"Thirties."

"165 pounds."

"Did he have an accent?"

"I guess so, but I never noticed it. You only notice accents on people you don't see every day."

"How old was he?"

"56."

"Young," she said. "That must make you nervous."

"Nervous, why?"

"Well, maybe it's a hereditary thing."

Leave it to a kid to make an already bad situation that much worse. Until she had mentioned it, it had never occurred to me that my father's early death might be something I might have to worry about as well. But after she said it, it was never far from my thoughts for the rest of the trip.

"Did you have brothers and sisters?"

"Did I? I'm not dead."

"Well, not *yet*," she said.

"No. No siblings," I said. "I don't think so, at least."

"How can you not know?" she asked, genuinely confused.

"Maybe there's one in Iran I don't know about."

"What's being an only child like?" she asked.

"It's great. No one scares you away from wearing sunscreen."

"You're a little sarcastic, aren't you?" she asked.

"That could be."

"What was your favorite thing about your father?" she asked.

"Two things: his sense of humor and his fearlessness."

The streets rolled beneath us like falling dominoes, the Haight vanishing behind us.

"Did he like to jump out of airplanes?"

"What? No, not that I know of."

"Did he ever swim with sharks?"

"I don't follow."

"Well, what made him fearless?"

"He would not have felt guilty about leaving a kid alone in San Francisco to find her way back to the BART station," I said, kidding her.

"I don't think he would have done that," she answered.

"No. My dad would have liked you," I said.

She smiled broadly and looked straight ahead. She liked that answer more than any of the others. I noticed that she hadn't said anything about her own father. I wondered why that was.

The driver let us out in front of an old apartment house that looked like something from a 1940s horror film, all Gothic spires and stone turrets.

"Jesus," I said. "Is it haunted?"

"Come on, Patrick," Dorothy said, laughing. "It's much nicer inside."

The lobby was lined with old Impressionist prints—Morisot, Pissarro, Gauguin, Renoir, Caillebotte—while the sculpture that stood in the center of the vintage space was a nude Diana aiming her arrow towards the skylight that was several stories high, a fact which gave the building the hybrid atmosphere specific to American interiors. We were a nation whose culture had always been a deeply democratic post-modernity, and nowhere was this more evident than in our nation's apartment houses, museum galleries, and downtown hubs: somehow every movement, every epoch of artistic, political, religious, architectural, and sexual practice and tradition somehow made its way out west, to the last frontier that existed on this earth, the place whose Holy Trinity was, on any given day, one as likely to be comprised of Frederick Douglass, John F. Kennedy, and Ella Fitzgerald as it was of old stalwarts like the Father, Son, and Holy Ghost.

The elevator was out of service, so I followed Dorothy to the stairway entrance in the eastern corner of the lobby, its door propped open with a well-placed brick, a disinterested security guard scrolling through his iPhone as we walked past his desk.

"We're on the third floor," Dorothy said. "You can see the TransAmerica Pyramid from our window. And the *Nudes Nudes Nudes* sign of the Condor Club just up the street," she added, giggling.

Her key wasn't halfway in the lock before the door swung open, and Dorothy was swept up in an embrace by a woman so breathlessly excited to see her safe and sound that it was almost impossible to see what the woman looked like. She was a living cartwheel: all swinging arms and legs, her hair falling across Dorothy's face like a modest waterfall, her lips kissing every inch of Dorothy's cheeks and head before finally stepping back and saying:

"You have the *worst* big sister in the world. The first thing I'm going to do tomorrow morning is go and buy us a couple of cell phones. And the next thing I'm going to do is beg you to forgive me."

Only then did she look up and notice that Dorothy was not alone. She gave the type of start that women in television comedies were always giving, as if the man who stood before them had suddenly appeared out of thin air, beamed in from the *Star Trek* soundstage, a modestly dressed man returned from battling an interstellar Klingon conspiracy.

"Hello," she said, looking down at Dorothy for a moment before returning her eyes to mine, and saying, for a second time,

"Hello."

Dorothy's sister had picked a good decade to romanticize. Everything about her, the long brown hair, the brown eyes, the thin tanned arms with a healthy dose of freckles, the flower print dress that went down to the floor, her bare feet peeking from the hemline like baby ducks underneath a mother's protective wing, was perfectly suited to the style of the 60s. She wore no make-up, her breasts were small (she, God bless her, wore no bra beneath her dress), and her slightly crooked nose had clearly been broken at some earlier time in her life. In other words, she was a lovely hippie, a girl who would have been at home in Woodstock, either on stage, singing like an angel in a flowing linen dress, or hanging out among the sprawling crowd, walking topless through the unwashed masses and handing out flowers to stoned peaceniks who thanked her for her kindness, a half-smoked joint dangling eternally from her parted, slightly chapped lips. She was like Joni Mitchell's younger sister, or Joan Baez's long-lost cousin, her thin neck and slight overbite making her just about the prettiest girl I had ever seen.

"Hello," I said. "I'm Patrick. I just wanted to make sure Dorothy got home safely." I didn't want to make her feel any worse than she already did.

"It's nice to meet you, Patrick," she said, shaking my hand. "Thank you so much for looking out for her."

Dorothy turned and hugged me, and then took my hand and said,

"Come on, Patrick. Let's show you our bachelorette pad."

"Yes, please," Gemma echoed. "Come in."

The apartment was a modest space that felt palatial because of the warmth with which it had been decorated: colored matte photographs of Woodstock hung on the wall, Jimi Hendrix in the middle of a guitar solo, plucking the electric notes of a new world order national anthem as naked revelers, their hair unkempt, bodies daubed with mud and grass, flowers held gently between their fingers and behind their ears, looked towards a sky that seemed to promise a much more beautiful world, as well as several psychedelic concert prints of late 60s shows by the Grateful Dead, the Jefferson Airplane, Creedence Clearwater Revival, Big Brother and the Holding Company, and Moby Grape, nearly all of them at Bill Graham's Fillmore West.

There were handmade quilts draped across the second-hand sofa, a glistening record player free-standing in a corner, and bookshelves made with bricks and boards that overflowed with works by Khalil Gibran, Alan Watts, Ken Kesey, Herman Hesse, Joan Didion, Hunter Thompson and the rest of the usual suspects. It was the kind of place where you could always feel comfortable putting your feet up on the table, and where you knew whatever food there was in the refrigerator would be enough to serve however many people had found their way inside on any given night.

In other words, it was the type of place that would produce a Dorothy Lewis, I thought to myself. A young kid with an unofficial doctorate in popular culture and progressive politics, a young kid who probably learned more in one afternoon with her beautiful older sister than she'd learn in an entire year of school.

"Have a seat," Gemma said, as she turned towards the small kitchen a few feet away. "Would you like some lemonade? A soda? I think I have some wine here somewhere."

"Lemonade would be perfect. Thank you."

Dorothy came to sit beside me, still beaming at being reunited with her sister, bumping her shoulder against mine for the second time that day.

"What started out as a pretty bad day has turned into a really good one, Patrick," Dorothy said.

And Gemma from the kitchen:

"So tell me what happened. How did you guys cross each other's paths? I was freaking out, worried that Dorothy would be all alone or…I don't even want to think about it," she said, as she carried a tall mug towards me, the sides designed with neon peace symbols and a silhouette of Mahatma Gandhi.

"It's hand-squeezed," she said. "I have some friends who work on an organic farm in Sausalito. They bring us fruit every time they cross the bridge to work the Farmer's Market on Sunday afternoons."

She stood there with an expectant smile on her face as I took my first sip.

"Well?"

"It's fantastic," I said. "Best lemonade I've ever had."

"Right?" she added. "There's nothing like it in the stores. You can really taste the difference when the lemons haven't been shot up with so many chemicals. There's plenty more if you want it," she said, moving towards the record player.

She knelt down and thumbed through some vinyl sleeves that were stacked at the bottom of the bookshelf.

A minute later she had made her choice, and a few seconds after that the opening chords of George Harrison's classic triple-LP, *All Things Must Pass,* were filling up the room, Harrison's voice never sounding warmer or lovelier.

Gemma sat across from us on a wooden chair that looked as if it were a sibling to the one Van Gogh had set aside for the imminent visit of Paul Gauguin. Both girls shared a crooked, exuberant smile that showed all of their teeth and lots of gum, as well as a wide-eyed, unblinking goodness that you could tell guaranteed that they would spend a lot of their time being hurt by insensitive people not smart enough to realize they were in the company of rare, special beauty. I had been with them for all of five minutes and already I never wanted to leave. *What was a silver medal?* I asked myself. Dad would understand. As much of a wandering spirit as he was, he would have understood being sidetracked by such goodness.

"Patrick doesn't like the Beatles," Dorothy teased. "He told me on the cab ride over here that they couldn't carry the Stones' luggage."

She was giggling as she said it.

"That is not true," I answered, feeling with every passing second that Dorothy Lewis was the little sister I never had.

"Don't let her suck you in," Gemma said. "It's taken me years to learn, Patrick. I'm telling you. This one here is a troublemaker."

Had the apartment been big enough for such a description, I would say that Gemma glided back into the kitchen, but in truth, she got up, smoothed her flowing skirt, and walked the six or seven steps it took to get back to the little room with a stove and sink. She had something cooking, even if she hadn't said what it was.

"The food will only be a few more minutes," she said.

It was my turn to get up.

"No, I don't want to put you two out like this. I should be going."

"Don't be ridiculous," Gemma said. "There's no way someone saves my sister and then doesn't at least get fed before being sent back out into the big, bad city. Our mother would never forgive us."

"It's true," Dorothy added. "Our mom was more Catholic than the Pope. If it got back to her that we let you continue your quest on an empty stomach, she'd be waiting at the gates, right there beside St. Peter when we were due to arrive, and she'd be shaking her head, totally disappointed in us."

"My Sweet Lord," Harrison's gentle, lovely paean to God, had begun to play. It was a track that made you believe in, at least, a life force, if not an outright higher power, whether or not you had ever set foot inside a church. Listening to this album—I hadn't heard it in several years— reminded me all over again that George Harrison might have been the single most underrated figure in rock and roll history, a man who was a part of the greatest band in pop history, and yet was stifled by the fact that two of his band-mates happened to be geniuses who only allocated two songs for him per record. That this was Gemma Lewis' go-to record only accelerated the fact that I was obviously already falling in love with her. Hand-squeezed lemonade and great pop music will do that to a man.

"And while we're waiting," Gemma began. "I do have an important question that must be asked: Beatles or Stones? Your life just might depend on the answer."

Chapter 4
A Tale of Two Orphans

"It depends," I said.

"Oh no," Gemma answered, leaning back in her chair, her arms lifted up above her head as if she were celebrating having scored the winning soccer goal in a World Cup match to reveal a pair of lovely armpits that hadn't been shaved in a couple of days. "That's not allowed. Absolutely not allowed. You have to decide. Desert Island time, you understand? Your plane has crashed, you're about to spend the next decade discovering your inner Robinson Crusoe, and all you have to choose from are either the noble lads from Liverpool or the bad boys of McMillan's London."

Gemma Lewis was like a living anti-depressant, a tablet of Lexapro with lovely breasts, and as I was pausing to give my answer the mock-dramatic weight I felt it needed, I wondered if she was wearing any underwear.

"Springsteen," I answered. They didn't say anything. I continued:

"Look, if I'm going to be stuck on a desert island for the next ten years, hunting wild boar with a bow and arrow constructed from the bark of an ancient palm tree, I want to make sure 'Thunder Road' and 'Darkness on the Edge of Town' are playing on the solar-powered stereo I have fashioned from the stray parts of the boat I wrecked."

"But," I continued. "If it's an England-only play-list, it's got to be the Beatles. There's never been a band as good as they were."

The room was filled with silence. After a dramatic pause of her own, Gemma said,

"You have chosen wisely."

Of course she was smiling as she said it. And then she winked at me, which practically caused me to levitate from the couch in excitement.

On the boulevard outside the sun had begun to set, and as we continued through side one of Harrison's musical tour de force, the girls continued their pop cultural interrogation.

"Oooh, this is fun," Gemma said. "Okay, Desert Island Books. Go."

"*The Great Gatsby. The Grapes of Wrath. Go Tell It On the Mountain. Their Eyes Were Watching God.*"

"Those are all American novels," Gemma answered.

"We do them better than anyone else. That and jazz music and illegally invading other countries."

"Movies."

"*The Sting. The Thief of Bagdad*, with Douglas Fairbanks. Any Pacino movie from the 1970s, especially *Serpico. Shampoo. Reds. Dick Tracy.*"

"Music."

"*Born to Run. Purple Rain.* Anything Billie Holiday. Anything Bob Dylan. Even his 80s stuff. Even his religious 80s stuff. *Songs in the Key of Life.*"

"Poetry."

"Whitman's *Leaves of Grass.* Edna St. Vincent Millay. Dylan Thomas. Langston Hughes."

"Painting."

"Klimt's *Danae.* Berthe Morisot's entire oeuvre. Winslow Homer's *The Cotton Pickers. Starry Night.* Anything by

Marc Chagall where there are flying lovers. Renoir's nudes, especially the redheads."

I felt like a contestant in a game show, the prize being that Gemma liked my cultural tastes enough to consider falling in love with me, or at least letting me make love to her relatively soon. What could I say? As a lifelong Giants fan, hope forever sprang eternal, no matter the length of the odds. Which, in my case, especially when it came to women, were considerable. David versus Goliath considerable. David with a sprained ankle, a torn meniscus in his kneecap, a case of mononucleosis considerable. A torn rotator cuff in his slingshot-wielding shoulder considerable. To be clear, it wasn't that women didn't find me charming or, even at times, in certain lighting, at very specific positions in the moon's trajectory, dashingly handsome. It was that to be in Gemma Lewis' presence was to feel like I was some Greek peasant who had stumbled onto shore just as Venus emerged in all her glory from that ocean-bearing oyster shell and thinking to himself, *I've got no shot here. None at all.*

Being out of tired metaphors for the moment, I took a breath to see if any more questions were forthcoming. The two sisters had apparently reached the deliberation stage. It had indeed become a game show, but instead of hoping for that double-decker yacht or even a souped-up Jaguar with chrome wheels, I merely wanted Gemma to like me. Sometimes life was just that simple.

"Well?" Dorothy asked Gemma, in a mock British voice. "Does he pass?"

"For the television audience at home," Gemma answered, "here are his following scores, 10 being the possible highest: he gets a 7 in the Literature Category. *Gatsby* was too predictable, and frankly, a little dated. *Grapes of Wrath* is overrated. Zora Neale Hurston is wonderful, but overall, our contestant is too rah-rah for American literature."

I had suddenly wandered onto a much more enjoyable version of *American Idol*. She crossed her legs, ran her hands back through her hair, smiled broadly and continued.

"He did really well in the movie category. He either has impeccable natural taste or he's been well-prepped. When we meet his parents someday, we'll know for sure…"

Dorothy looked at me for a moment, worried Gemma had accidentally ruined the moment. I smiled at Dorothy, shaking my head slightly to tell her not to worry.

"Warren Beatty remains my all-time favorite actor, along with the ever-handsome Sean Connery. *The Sting* is a classic. Al Pacino in *Serpico* proved a man could be an honest cop and yet retain his hippie spirit. The fact that I've never heard of the *Baghdad* movie means it is either a silent or a foreign film. Which means our handsome contestant is cultured.

"He stumbled a little in the music category, registered a 5 out of a possible 10. Prince remains the only man I've ever seen who can look gorgeous in a pompadour and stiletto heels—the man's got a better butt than I do—but every time I hear a Springsteen song the only thing it makes me wonder is whether my car is due for an oil change. Billie Holiday was good but she was no Ella Fitzgerald. And no Janis Joplin, no Joan Baez, no Grateful Dead. These are things that can't be forgiven."

"No Grateful Dead," Dorothy echoed. "That one really hurt him."

"*But*…You more than made up for such a poor showing in the music category with your showing in the poetry and art categories: Walt Whitman, Chagall, Morisot. A combined 9.5 in those two. The only thing that kept you from a perfect score was your omission of Mary Oliver. Had you mentioned her, you would have been an instant member into Gemma's Hall of Fame." She paused, looking towards the small dining room table tucked into the even smaller alcove by the large window that opened out onto Columbus Avenue. "As it is, I'd say you've earned your pizza."

She rose and walked into the kitchen. Dorothy winked at me, softly clapped her hands and whispered to me, "She likes you."

We sat around the table for the next two hours telling stories: we talked about our parents, the cities we grew up in, what we thought of Obama, whether the Catholic Church was still worth believing in, why the album Bob Dylan and the Grateful Dead recorded together was as awful as it was, and what to make of the Giants' pitching staff, especially the mercurial Barry Zito, who on some nights looked like he still had plenty left in the tank but who most of the time looked like his best days were certainly behind him.

The pizza was magnificent: thin crust, apple slices, red onions, heirloom tomato chunks, three different types of mozzarella cheese, and a dash of garlic combined to make a classic in Italian cuisine. Luckily Gemma had made two of them. We washed them down with ice water, freshly squeezed lemonade, and a bottle of Coca Cola that we passed around like a trio of horse-track winos too drunk to even consider using actual glasses.

At 6pm I knew that I needed to go, unless I wanted to lose an entire day in my search.

Dorothy held my hand as I walked to the door, and gave me a hug before stepping back and saying,

"This was one of the most unexpectedly great days I've ever had, Patrick. Right up there with the night my mother took Gemma and me to see a midnight screening of the original *Superman* on the big screen at the Clay Theater back when we were living in Pacific Heights. I don't care what anyone says, there was only one Superman, and his name was Christopher Reeve. And the day…You know what? I'll save the rest of this for later, Patrick. I know we'll see you again. Good luck with your quest," she said, tapping my shoulders with a spatula she had grabbed from the coffee table, a middle school queen blessing an unexpected knight.

"Sweetie," Gemma said, grabbing a coat. "I'm going to walk downstairs with Patrick, okay? You start washing the dishes. I'll be right back."

We walked in silence down the hallway, both of us reaching for the elevator button at the same time, our hands momentarily meeting. We still hadn't spoken by the time the doors opened.

Inside Gemma turned to me, and said,

"You really did save Dorothy today, you know? She may seem confident, and she's definitely brilliant, but she doesn't like being alone, especially since our mother died. I never should have taken her to the rally today," she said, shaking her head. "It was a stupid thing to do."

"You're being too hard on yourself," I answered. "You think she would have let you go without her? You're her moon and sun, Gemma, She'll follow you anywhere. You take good care of her. The best. She's a lucky girl."

The doors opened, and we stepped into the empty foyer, the colored silence of all those Impressionist prints providing an oddly pastoral tenor to our walk.

At the revolving doors I turned, extended my hand, and said, "Thank you for the wonderful dinner. I owe you one."

Gemma blushed slightly, looked past me into the street for a moment, and met my hand in a shake. As she turned to walk away I pulled her back to me, her face inches from my own, and leaned in and kissed her.

After a few seconds I withdrew, returned her gaze, and smiled with an ease that belied the rush of adrenaline I was feeling inside.

"I'll be seeing you," I said.

I turned and walked through the orbit of the decades-old double doors. By the time I looked back from my place on the sidewalk, Gemma was walking back towards the elevator.

For the entirety of the cab ride I felt like Gemma and I had just entered the pantheon of truly great, spontaneous first kisses, on par with Tom Cruise kissing Kelly McGillis at the side of the road in *Top Gun*, Burt Lancaster making out with Deborah Kerr in the surf in *From Here to Eternity*, or even that returning naval vet kissing the nurse in a euphoric Times Square on VJ Day, 1945. I had cracked the make-out Hall of Fame, which had me floating by the time I stepped out of the cab in front of St. Ignatius Cathedral.

I paid the driver and walked towards the Rectory.

I knocked on the door and waited.

And waited.

After three or four minutes it became clear that the Catholic priests were operating on Post Office Time—any visit made after 5pm was going to be met with shuttered doors—and that it was likely that I was going to have to come back in the morning if I wanted to talk to either them or the secretaries that manned the front offices.

Not wanting to throw in the towel for the evening so easily, however, I decided to walk down to the Cathedral proper, and see if there were any priests hearing evening confessions for those whom—insomniac or otherwise—only had time to make it to church when everyone else was already safely home and eating dinner in front of their television sets for the night.

The church had double-wooden doors, the type with dual wrought iron handles that looked like they dated back to the Middle Ages, when the Church was still heavily invested in burning witches and invading middle eastern countries in order to more fully secure God's grace. Inside there was the kind of silence that only the interior of a church possesses. A silence possessed of the echoes, undertones, and resonant melodies emanating from a two-story organ that, though it stands silent at the front of the church, still lets its presence be known, as if it were an outsized player piano who knew part of its power was that its songs were heard even when it was supposed to be off for the night.

There were about eight or ten individuals spread across the sprawling aisles of the church, a few of them homeless men who had found a warm place to sleep through the late afternoons and the evenings so that, when they were expelled back out onto the streets come nightfall, they could have their wits about them through the hours of darkness that held a cavalcade of possible dangers: drunken thrill-seekers set on taking out their vitriol and self-loathing on the vulnerable, drug-addicted vagrants who heard voices, saw ghosts and felt devils where there were none, graveyard-shift patrol cops whose hearts had been hardened by the suffering they had seen over the years, a hardness that enabled them to roust the homeless from their makeshift beds and tents and cardboard-and-newspaper constructed yurts even though these men clearly had no other place to go. There was a young couple in their mid-twenties, their heads bowed in the pew closest to the empty altar, a looming, levitating Christ above them, who, from where I was, seemed to look down on them with a sensitivity that only a great artist could convey. Elsewhere there was an old man reading through the liturgy, a middle-aged woman lighting candles in an alcove where Mary reigned supreme, and a handful of teenagers who were holding hands in front of a statue of St. Francis, that noblest and most holy of men.

At the farthest end of an aisle six or seven rows from the front, there was a priest, Latino, his full head of hair gone silver, his skin like that of an ex-Merchant Marine who had spent decades exposed to salt and sun and wind, speaking with another man of roughly the same age, well-dressed, in a sharp and finely tailored black suit, both of their voices suitably low.

I walked farther down the aisle and took a seat toward the middle of the church, far enough away from the two conversing men to give them the privacy they deserved, but close enough to make sure the priest wouldn't slip away without me having a chance to speak with him.

As I sat and waited for the men to finish talking, I thought about the service we had had for my father only a few days' prior, held in Ithaca Park, a beachside preserve nestled on a small set of rolling hills in North Laguna Beach, a stone's throw from the famed Main Street basketball courts and the downtown lighthouse that dated back to the first year of the Coolidge administration, as assorted family and friends came to eat Iranian food (courtesy of a local place owned by a friend of my father's) and share memories of some of my father's more colorful stories and adventures. I thought about how he and I had rarely, if ever, spoken in a meaningful way about religion. No, let me rephrase that. We talked a lot about religion, about what Christ might have actually been capable of doing—my father felt that it was possible, likely even, that Christ was no miracle worker, but instead a pre-modern Einstein, a man who had figured out a way to tap into those unused but wildly potential-filled components of his brain and accomplish things (walking on water, for instance) that weren't magical so much as they required an intellectual facility no one else had been able to access. We talked about the myriad ways in which organized religion stripped faith of its most beauteous, imaginative, restorative functions (one of his favorite books was Dostoyevsky's *The Brothers Karamazov,* particularly the Grand Inquisitor section, where a group of priests jail the returned Christ because they know that if they acknowledge he is truly the Son of God, they will be out of a job), and we talked about the ways in which the writers of the Bible and the Koran were possessed of a poetic and imagistic brilliance that only Shakespeare, and maybe Cervantes, were capable of matching (I would have added Bob Dylan, but Dad never got into American popular music). But we never talked about our own core beliefs, and as I sat in the pew of this church where he and my mother were married nearly forty years prior, I found myself not only praying for him, but praying *to* him, an act that, frankly, surprised me. Indeed, I had come to this church looking for an old friend of my father's, and instead I had found myself aware that I was in the presence of my actual father: I imagined him sitting in the pew next to me, his shoes off, his slacks and collared shirt and tie still on, the glasses that he had begun to wear in his mid-40s perched classily across the upper bridge of his nose, ready to talk and listen and laugh with his only child in the way that we used to do so often, in an era that seemed almost dreamlike to me now. Though it is true that I have always liked to sit in empty, or almost empty, churches, mostly because they are some of the most beautiful spaces in modern America, that time was different: it was the first time I had understood that a church could be not only portal, but a symbolic, spiritualist, interstellar United Nations: come in, sit down, state your country of birth. The ghosts of your ancestors will be with you shortly.

A few minutes later the well-dressed man said his goodbyes, and I got up and began walking towards the gracious, though also clearly fatigued, priest.

"Excuse me, sir," I said, now only three or four feet away from him. "Can I speak with you for a minute?"

He nodded.

"I'm Patrick Karimi," I extended my hand. "I'm looking for Father Jim O'Leary."

The priest met my handshake warmly, offering a firm grip in return.

"Good to meet you, Patrick. I'm Ray," he answered. "Father O'Leary retired about five years ago."

"Do you know how I might get in touch with him?"

Father Ray guided us to a set of pews. We sat down. Ray had the voice of a long-time smoker, a voice that would have gone perfectly on a grizzled detective in an old 30s hard-boiled homicide series featuring a south-of-the-border transplant cracking wise on the streets of old Los Angeles. It struck me that his voice must have been an enormous bonus while delivering his sermons—it was a voice you *wanted* to listen to, a voice whose weathered strength implied that its owner had experienced the types of things he was speaking about (and often warning against), a voice which provided the authenticity that far too many men of the cloth were lacking, America's present Archbishop and the current Pope included.

"How do you know Father O'Leary?" Father Ray asked.

Over the next three of four minutes I recounted the story of my father's friendship with the old priest, and why it was that I had come looking for him after so many years.

"Soccer player, eh?" he said. "I could never get into it. They should be able to use their hands."

He laughed deeply again, and continued.

"Yeah, I still see him now and then. He's a big Giants fan. Of course, who isn't around here? We go to a game once or twice a year, usually when the Yankees or the Red Sox are in town. And once in a while we'll run into each other at the VA or down at General. Priests are like mobsters. Once you're in, you never get out," he said, his low rumble of a laugh sounding like an approaching subway car.

"Tonight's a game night, so if he's not at Clancy's South of Market, he'll be at his place, out near The Presidio. I'll write you the address, but you won't really need it."

"Why not?"

"Because he lives in the only completely blue house in all of San Francisco. It's awful. I've been telling him to paint it for years."

Chapter 5
A Sport and a Pastime

He looked like a cross between a former prizefighter—the kind who had made up for his lack of natural talent and middling punching power with a heart that simply refused to let him go down—and an aged mystic in a Sophocles production, the grizzled seer who doles out truths from a hidden lair-cave somewhere beyond the outskirts of the plague-ridden city. He wore black pants, black slip-on dress shoes, a black button-down shirt with the collar open, and a black scarf around his modest shoulders like a cotton version of the middleweight belt he had, in an alternate universe, successfully defended six decades earlier. He had to be nearing eighty years old, but he looked sixty, sixty-five at the most. He stood roughly five-feet-eight inches, was probably within five pounds of the weight he'd been when he'd said his first mass, and, like Father Ray, had a complexion that made it clear he had spent a fair share of time beside the sea.

He recognized me immediately.

"You're not as good-looking as your father, that handsome bastard," Jim O'Leary said, not two seconds after he opened the door. "But you probably do all right for yourself."

He stood to the side, held the door open with his left hand. I was surprised that he didn't seem at all startled to see Hassan Karimi's son standing on his front steps.

"Come on in, Patrick. The game's about to start."

It was the second apartment I had entered that day, and it was every bit as welcoming as the first, the only difference being that if Gemma and Dorothy's place was a paean to a bygone era of paisley and psychedelia, Father Jim O'Leary's place looked as if he were living inside a satellite wing of the lost library of Alexandria. Epic tomes were stacked on high shelves, and plenty more rose up from the carpet like paperback beanstalks.

Everyone was accounted for: St. Augustine, Meister Eckhart, Richard Wright, F. Scott Fitzgerald, both Wordsworths, all three Brontes, Einstein, Chinua Achebe, Toni Morrison, Dylan Thomas, Robert Frost, the Confessional Poets, David Halberstam, John F. Kennedy's *Profiles in Courage*, an entire shelf devoted to the Middle Eastern Ecstatics, Rumi and Hafiz and Saadi and Ferdusi— "your father sent me the Hafiz," Jim said as I scanned names and titles—Sappho, Churchill, Gabriel Garcia Marquez, James Baldwin, Rumer Godden, Isabel Allende, Wislawa Szymborska, and on and on.

"You want something to drink?" he asked.

"I'd love a glass of water. Thanks."

"Have a seat," he said, as he walked towards the cramped kitchen space. "There hasn't been a Karimi here since your mother came to visit about fifteen years ago. We went to an exhibition at the De Young of the Hudson River Valley painters. Your mother loved them. Had I been a wealthy man I would have bought every single one of those paintings on the walls, all the Thomas Coles and Frederic Edwin Churchs I could carry and given them to her as a present," he said. "I've never seen anyone who loved art the way your mother does," he added.

"It's true," I said. "She took me to Las Vegas when I was eight or nine years old. We spent the whole time at the art museum and at some of the galleries that the fancy hotels featured. We had every place to ourselves, basically. I don't think anyone else even knew those places existed. On our way out of town we stopped off in this little church, and as we walked in, she said, 'Make sure you say a prayer for all the men who gambled away enough money to buy those Van Goghs and Monets we saw, sweetheart. That was nice of them to do.'"

"Your father was playing out of his league with that girl," Jim said. "And he knew it, even though he never acted like it."

Jim paused, the expression on his face changing from one of relaxed nostalgia to sincere concern. He had gone from being a kind old uncle to a conscientious priest in a little under a second.

"Are your parents well?"

"Mom is wonderful," I answered. "She's in Europe right now. Her first time abroad. She's probably sleeping in the D'Orsay Museum, actually, instead of in the hotel I booked for her. But Dad died last week. In his sleep. Heart attack."

Jim settled slowly back into his seat, an act that for the first time since I had arrived illustrated the toll the advancing years had taken on his body.

"Same old Hassan," he said. "Always full of surprises. I figured he'd die at 125 in a parachuting accident."

I wasn't surprised that nearly everyone I'd informed of my father's death couldn't get over the news that he had died in his sleep. It was proof that I wasn't the only one who saw him as a mythic, immortal figure.

Jim returned from the kitchen with a glass of water for me and a glass of wine for himself.

"Have a seat, Son. This is the era of the multi-task. We can talk about your father and watch a ballgame at the same time."

"Now this team is the opposite of your father," he transitioned, raising the glass to his lips. "They're seventeen games out of first place, their best player is on the DL and their manager will likely be fired at season's end. This is not a team that is going to surprise anyone. They lose the same way every night: awful pitching backed up by anemic hitting. This team was born in last place."

"Well," I answered. "At least you have the Raiders," in reference to possibly the most dysfunctional franchise in all of professional sports.

"The Raiders," he answered, taking another swig, "make the West Bank look hopeful by comparison."

The game that was about to start was one of the hundreds of meaningless regular season baseball contests that had no significance other than the fact that it was on the schedule, and therefore had to be played. The hometown Giants were playing the New York Yankees, otherwise known to baseball fans outside of New York as the Evil Empire, a franchise whose payroll was larger than the combined payrolls of half the league, a franchise run for most of the last thirty years by the late George Steinbrenner, professional sports' version of Richard Nixon, a mean-spirited, wildly temperamental paranoid who once paid a mobster to dig up embarrassing information on his best player (Dave Winfield) after Steinbrenner and Winfield had fallen out, and who, keeping with the spirit of Tricky Dick, was once suspended by the Commissioner's Office for illegally contributing to one of Nixon's countless slush funds during the swindling free-for-all that was the thirty-seventh Presidential Administration. The Yankees were a franchise that had won a record twenty-seven baseball championships, and who, a few months later, would go on to win the 2009 title behind the second coming of a murderer's row lineup that included future Hall of Famers Derek Jeter, Alex Rodriguez, and Mark Texeira. The Giants, on the other hand, were still a year away from their first World Series title in over fifty years. In other words, it wasn't shaping up to be a fair fight.

Oh, and Barry Zito was pitching, a former All-Star who had spent the past several years struggling to rekindle his earlier glories.

"This could be ugly," I said.

Father O'Leary only nodded in response, given that he was midway through a whispered, only half-joking prayer,

"Our Father, who art in Heaven, blessed be thy name...deliver us from A-Rod...and pitch around Teixeira...Amen."

When Jim finished, he began talking again, neither of us turning our heads from the game, which began with Zito throwing a strike to the swinging Curtis Granderson.

"Atta boy, Barry," Jim O'Leary encouraged, like a supportive grandfather sitting in the bleachers for his grandson's high school game.

"He *did* win the Cy Young six years ago," I said. "So he's got it in him."

"I like your optimism. Take that faith into the streets," he said, emphasizing his point with a little pump of his fist, as if he were a rookie pinch-hitter celebrating his first home run while rounding third.

"What's the point?" I asked rhetorically, reaching for my glass of water. "No one's listening anymore anyway."

"That's not the point. That's not the point at all." There was a rhythm to his speech, the rhythm of a man who'd spent his life sermonizing from the pulpit. He knew the power of repetition. Of short, clipped language possessed of an understated lyricism.

"You don't worry about whether they care or not. *You* care. That's what matters."

He paused for breath as Zito struck Granderson out on a nasty curve that looked less like a baseball than a boomerang, angling down to Granderson's ankles as he swung.

"Beautiful," Jim said, the two of us high-fiving.

"What's that Yeats line?" I asked. "And everywhere…"

"And everywhere the ceremony of innocence is drowned, for the best lack conviction, and the worst are full of a passionate intensity."

"A Catholic priest quoting the greatest of all Protestant poets. I like it," I said.

"And giving shelter to a young Muslim man sleeping on a bench in Golden Gate Park nearly forty years ago," he added. "It's not a matter of knowing the Gospels by heart, or following the Commandments on a daily basis."

"Careful," I said, "You sound like a man angling to be ex-communicated."

"I'm retired. They can't get me now," he winked.

"I was only kidding you," I said.

"I know that," he answered. "But still. You think what I did all those years, and what I still do, has much of anything to do with the Church? You think I'm carrying out the orders of the Pope? That isn't how it works. Do you turn your back on your country because you don't like the President? Or because you think some of our laws are unjust?"

"That's a good point."

"That's the only point. The Pope? He's a bureaucrat. He doesn't represent the Church any more than Bush or Obama represent America."

Zito threw one high and inside to Derek Jeter, brushing the Yankees' captain back off the plate, sending him into the dirt to avoid being hit by a fastball that clocked in at ninety-seven miles per hour on the gun.

"Wow," Jim O'Leary exclaimed. "Zito thinks its 2002 all over again," referring to the year Zito won the coveted Cy Young award. "He hasn't hit that speed on the radar gun since he was twenty-five years old and playing for Oakland."

Jim clapped his hands together, nodded his head in my direction, and took another extended drink of his wine.

"You're a writer, son. I've read your books. All those poems about love and daydreams and world peace. You're writing little gospels, stuff that tries to remind everyone there is a beauty to this world that isn't here by coincidence. That the grace of some guiding hand has painted us into being like some gigantic fresco."

"Norman Mailer's belief was that God was an artist, not a lawmaker," I affirmed.

"Norman Mailer? Here I am trying to talk to you about the essential sanctity of human life and you're quoting a guy who once stabbed his wife."

Jeter had patiently worked Zito into a full-count, and the home crowd rose and cheered as Zito took the signal from his catcher.

"He's going to throw a sinker here," Jim said. "It's his out pitch."

A sinker it was. Jeter was caught looking at a ball that went from twelve to six in a tenth of a second.

"Keep predicting those kinds of things and you'll make a believer out of me," I said.

"It isn't about believing. It's about accepting. Look at what you're doing. You're fulfilling the desires of your father, trying to complete something which he didn't get a chance to do himself…"

I started to speak, but he waved me away.

"By doing so you acknowledge that life has meaning, that there is a narrative that you must be faithful to."

"It could be a meaning that we create."

"And where do you get a sense of what that 'meaning' might be? It's latent within you. It was inside of you before you were even born. You read your King Arthur as a child, right? You know the sword in the stone? What is the significance of that story?"

"It's a narrative about fate. That there is a preordained destiny the individual possesses that he is fated to fulfill."

Wasn't it?

"Yes. So who created this destiny? Who led Arthur to that sword?"

"You think God led him there," I said.

"You speak of God the way six-year-old children do. The way they show him in movies. A bearded man in a white robe who looks like Gandalf's older brother. But yes, God *did* lead him there."

"But that's not the God I want to believe in. A God who plays favorites."

"No," Father O'Leary answered, vigorously shaking his head from side to side. "You're wrong. It isn't a matter of God, as you have put it, 'playing favorites.' He isn't Santa Claus. He has completed his canvas, as your buddy Mailer says, and now that canvas belongs to the world. It isn't his anymore. It hasn't been in a long, long time."

He paused to watch Zito have a quick conference with his catcher, Bengie Molina, one of a trio of brothers who were currently calling signals from behind the plate for major league teams. All of them were of a type: tough-minded, deeply cerebral, and slow-as-molasses. Watching each of them run the bases was like watching evolution. It seemed to take centuries just for them to make it to first.

"You want people to respect what you write? You want to people to extract meaning from your novels? Well, God demands the same care and attention. He gave us one painting, but it's a good one, the best we have, and you as a fellow artist owe it to its creator to try to protect what he gave us. So when you say 'nobody cares,' you're missing the point."

He clapped his hands again, took the last drink of his wine and rose to get another from the kitchen.

"I'm getting one for you too. No man is going to understand what we're talking about while drinking a glass of water. It just isn't possible."

By the time he returned Zito had fallen behind in the count, 2-0, to Alex Rodriguez, the most feared hitter in the American League, a three-time MVP only a few months away from turning in one of the most storied postseasons in Major League history, when it seemed like every time the thirty-two-year-old slugger had come to the plate it was a foregone conclusion that a home run was imminent.

"Oh no," Jim said. "This isn't good."

"He's going to have to throw inside on this pitch or the next," I added. "And A-Rod doesn't miss many of those."

"Well, Zito has looked sharp so far. Maybe he can pull himself out of this," Jim said, as Zito threw a fastball so far outside of the strike zone that it landed somewhere in Oakland.

"Wild pitch," the announcer deadpanned.

"You think so?" Jim asked.

Both of us were leaning forward, our eyes squinting as we focused on the television, two grown men who had taken a timeout from a discussion on the mysteries of creation to focus on something even more important: baseball.

Zito shook off three signals from Molina before finally finding a pitch call to his liking.

As he started into his wind-up, Zito subtly dropped his glove and reared his leg up towards the sky, a leg-kick so pronounced it looked like the pitcher was auditioning for a role in the San Francisco Opera House's production of *Swan Lake*, Zito's lanky frame contorting itself into an evolving pretzel that had been famous, in his prime, for paralyzing batters just long enough for them to have been a millisecond late in swinging at the pitch.

It was a nasty fastball. 98 on the gun. Straight down the heart of the plate, Rodriguez swinging so hard he lost his balance and fell to a knee as he tried vainly to catch up with it.

"DON'T HURT 'EM BARRY!" Father Jim O'Leary exclaimed, pumping both of his fists, holding out his hand for another high-five from me as A-Rod tried to regain his bearings.

"He does know it isn't 2002, doesn't he?" I asked.

"Forget about 2002," Jim responded. "That looked more like Sandy Koufax in *1962*."

Moments later, after A-Rod foul-tipped a pitch out-of-play behind home plate, Zito had taken the slugger back to a full-count.

"This guy is going to give me a heart attack," Jim said, as Zito nodded at Molina's signal.

Another fastball. This one a cutter, breaking across the plate like a BART car going off the tracks. A-Rod took a swing that, had it connected, would have put the ball somewhere outside of Phoenix, but it didn't, and instead the league's best player found himself walking back towards the dugout.

Zito had gotten through two innings, including the heart of the Yankee order, without giving up a hit. It had been the type of performance that, so far at least, always reminded me of why I was a sports fan: every time you watched a game, there was always the chance of seeing something special.

Chapter 6
The Soldier

By the fifth inning we were starting to realize that something special might have been happening at the ballpark: Zito had fanned six straight batters, including an exhilarating three-pitch strikeout of Robinson Cano, a young Yankee star whose bat speed was so quick it often seemed like he had time to swing twice at pitches before the ball crossed the plate.

"I'm with you," Jim said, unable to hide his elation. "He's turning back the clock tonight."

"Crazy, it's like he's inhabiting the body of Cy Young right now. That last pitch to Cano hit 102 on the gun. He's *never* hit 102 on the gun. And there was so much movement on that pitch that a cop could have ticketed it for excessive lane changes," I said.

We spent another inning talking around what we were both thinking: we might be in the process of watching a no-hitter. But of course, being the old-school baseball fans that we were—and being the superstitious Catholics that we would always be—there was no way we were going to acknowledge such a possibility out loud. That would be a break of fan protocol along the lines of walking out onto the infield with a blowtorch and a can of gasoline and setting fire to the grass. No, we marveled at Zito's control, at his movement, at the stunning velocity of his pitches, but we refused to actually utter the words: *No-No.*

It was an 0-2 count in the top of the sixth to Jeter when the telephone rang.

The receiver Jim spoke into looked like it might have been the one Alexander Graham Bell had in his guest room, something that should have been in a museum by then rather than the living room of an actual human being. But then again, Father Jim O' Leary clearly did things his own way.

Jim kept squinting at the screen while delivering short yesses and uh-uhs to whoever was on the other end of the telephone, looking my way and nodding excitedly when Jeter grounded out on a weak dribbler to third, pumping his fist to let me know he was still invested in the game at hand.

He ended the brief call by saying, "I'll be there in twenty minutes," and promptly replaced the receiver back onto its antiquated body.

"What's going on?" I asked, aware that it had to be something serious to merit Jim leaving in the middle of a prospective no-hitter.

"I've got to go and pick up a friend. You want to come along?" he asked, grabbing his coat from the hallway closet.

"Sure."

He threw me the keys.

"You'll like the car," he said, grinning like a sly college kid who has just succeeded in stealing a rival mascot. "It's a 1994 BMW I found at a police auction for 800 dollars. Cornering in that thing makes you feel like you're at the Daytona 500. Don't hesitate to let the clutch out on her a bit. St. Christopher will make sure we have nothing but green lights all the way to the Heights tonight."

99

Driving at night in San Francisco is one of the more magical experiences you can have in life. Given that most of the high-end tech firms, Wall Street corporate headquarters, and art galleries have all closed by six o'clock at the latest, and given that the BART is the preferred means of travel for the nighthawks who spend their nights bar-hopping South of Market or dining in the upscale eateries in Pacific Heights, the streets are relatively deserted, and you are left to coast through a labyrinthine landscape that is even more gorgeous in the fog and moonlight of the darkness than it is during the kind of glorious, sunny summer day that it had been only a few hours earlier.

Jim was right. The car more than lived up to BMWs classic tag line: The Ultimate Driving Machine. No kidding. A buddy of mine who had done two tours in Iraq over the past decade had once told me that you didn't want to be caught on a desert straightaway outside of Baghdad behind the wheel of anything other than Europe's finest. At the time, I had chalked it up to a military-version of western snobbishness, if not also a humorous example that even young men as serious as those serving in uniform could not entirely divest themselves of the boys-with-toys ethos that every male, regardless of cultural background or political affiliation, possesses. But that night, driving an aging, baseball-addicted priest across a cityscape as demanding as any driver could conceive, I could not have imagined a better car to be driving in. I felt like I was piloting a hovercraft across the Mississippi River, or a submarine through international waters, as silent and as stealth as the one Clark Gable commanded in *Run Silent, Run Deep*. In other words, this was one hell of a car.

"I told you," Jim said, reaching over to turn on the radio.

A second later the car was filled with the sounds of Nat King Cole in his supper-club era prime: "Mona Lisa," one of the finest songs the Windy City's chosen son ever recorded. Immediately it felt like the drive Jim and I were taking had gone from a modest sojourn to a noble quest.

"Nice call," I said. "An American classic."

"I met him once," Jim said. "Back in '61. There was a rally in downtown L.A. Someone had burned a cross on Nat's lawn earlier that year when he had moved into some high-end neighborhood, Bel Air or Hancock Park. One of those places where the only people of color were the ones that did the gardening. Nat's drummer had a cousin who had been in the seminary with me. I wound up spending an hour or so in a hotel room before the rally with that cousin, the drummer, Nat, Tom Bradley, and Robert Kennedy.

"That's some company," I said, turning left at a stoplight.

"Yeah, I was thirty-two years old. I'd been a priest for less than a year and there I was in a room with a handful of all-timers. I'll never forget it," Jim said, looking out the window and onto the lamp-lit streets. It was Jim's Bob-Dylan-in-Golden-Gate-Park moment, I could tell. Everyone deserves to get at least one of those in their lives.

"So where are we headed, anyway?" I asked.

Jim leaned back, removed his glasses and began to wipe them with the hem of his coat.

"Bobby's been back for about six months. Three tours. The last one was bad. Of the nineteen men in his platoon, thirteen died in combat. One died of a virus. They

101

could never figure out what it was. In the first month back, two more took their own lives, and another was arrested for armed robbery. Bobby seems to be unable to make up his mind as to whether he wants to die or go to prison."

"How old is he?"

"He'll be twenty-two next month. His mother took her first communion with me. I gave the sermon at his father's funeral. His grandfather's too. He's the closest thing I've ever had to a son," Jim said, his voice steady, his glasses back on.

Jim leaned over and turned the volume up on the radio. He shut his eyes and leaned back in his seat. We drove the rest of the way in silence, the voice of Nat King Cole serenading us as we, per Jim's prediction, hit all the greens.

We were driving through an area lined by the classic old Victorian homes of the Haight-Ashbury District, the storied crossroads where Jerry Garcia, rather than selling his soul to the devil for musical genius, got the devil stoned on some high-end LSD and then took the talents he needed before the devil came to.

The area had gone through that most American of changes: Gentrification. All around us were upscale vintage clothiers who had muscled out the low-brow smoke-and-bead shops that had once been staples of the region, which, when combined with the fact that it often seemed like every teenaged dropout from Boston to Tucson somehow found his way here, gave the area one of the more uniquely paradoxical, schizophrenic urban personalities I had ever seen. But no matter: the place still retained a substantive magic that no amount of superficial glamour or devastating lack could change. This was where the Free Love movement had most fully flowered, these streets were the ones where it once seemed that a new America was more than a mere possibility, and there were moments when, if one listened closely enough, the music of the era, the great LPs of Janis Joplin and Big Brother and the Holding Company and the Jefferson Airplane and Creedence Clearwater Revival and Otis Redding and Moby Grape could still be heard playing softly on the autumn winds, plugged into the muted amplifier of an almost-full California moon.

"Turn left here," Jim said.

A moment later,

"It's on the right-hand side at the end of this block. Park where you can."

The amount of time I had spent inside of police stations—not including the field trip my first-grade class took to the local precinct when I was six years old—was zero, unless you counted the hundreds of hours I had spent watching old *Miami Vice* reruns on cable. But Jim clearly was a regular: two plainclothesmen greeted him by name as they walked by us in the lobby, and the duty secretary knew him well enough to say to him:

"During a possible no-no too." She shook her head. "That boy owes you."

"It's good to see you, Delia," Jim answered, clearly used to her ribbing. "Is he all right?"

"Depends on what you mean by 'all right.' One of these times he's not going to make it out alive," Delia answered, her accent placing her somewhere outside of Pittsburgh. I could practically hear the tides of the Monongahela River in her voice. "They're bringing him up now."

"Thank you, dear," Jim said, tapping his fingers decisively on the counter before turning towards the worn sofa that had been placed against the far wall of the lobby. We took a seat.

Five minutes later the electronic door opened from inside. The swoosh reminded me of the suction sound I had always imagined Melville's whale made in the moment before it first attacked the Pequod.

Bobby Robicheaux was an old twenty-one. I had seen men like him in the night classes that I sometimes taught, where young vets trying to transition back into normal lives would sit towards the back of the classroom and try not to let the ghosts get the better of them. As I got to know those former soldiers over the semesters, many of them told me enough about their experiences overseas for me to know they were more than simply battle-hardened toughs: they were exhausted, strung-out Spartans, members of a military stretched so thin that it kept calling back its best and brightest for yet another tour while the rest of us sat the whole damned thing out. We had created an entire generation of reverse Prodigal Sons (and Daughters): men and women who wanted to come home but whose country refused to let them.

Jim rose and walked towards him. I stood but lingered near the vending machines, scanning the colored aisles of candy bars and potato chips as if they were the waiting souls of the incarcerated, and that all Bobby Robicheaux needed to do was put $1.75 into the coin slots, enter the holding number of his spirit, say, B10, and his soul would be delivered by way of the electronic mechanism back into his waiting hands.

I hung back for a few moments as the two men, one who had eased into old age, and one who had been prematurely thrust into it, talked as they moved towards the door, and then walked towards the door myself when I knew they were already outside.

After descending the steps Jim introduced us.

"Patrick Karimi, Bobby Robicheaux. Patrick's a Lakers fan, Bobby. Try not to hold it against him."

We shook hands, Bobby looking somewhere above my right shoulder, as if there might be snipers on the rooftops beyond him.

"You two sit up front," Jim said. "The old man needs to stretch his legs a bit."

"Where to?" I asked.

"Make a left at the next light," Jim said. "It's not too far from here."

It reminded me of the graveyard off the 5 Freeway in Los Angeles where my mother's sister was buried, the kind of cemetery that is standard east-coast fare but an aberration out west: tombstones jutting out of the ground at odd angles like stalled dominoes unsure of which direction to fall, trees so weighted down by the burden of branches and leaves that they looked like lush, oversized scarecrows, futilely attempting to scare death from the premises, old wrought iron fences bordering the property's perimeter like rusted holdovers from some old Victorian novel where the reader was immediately aware there were spirits about who refused to stay under the ground.

For the average thirty-four-year-old American, I had experienced what I felt like was a lot of death: the suicides of four close friends, a car accident that took the lives of three others, a heroin overdose at the age of fourteen that claimed the still-fledgling life of a neighborhood buddy I used to trade baseball cards with, the shooting of a friend in college that was never solved, as well as the more common occurrences of old relatives passing away and teaching colleagues who had succumbed to cancer. And yet in all of those experiences I was still largely a witness, a theatergoer given a window into death's bazaar, where the lives and hearts and dreams of so many that I knew were on display and yet could not be purchased back—in other words, I was a voyeur peering, however unwillingly, into the abyss but ever-aware I had the luxury of pulling back from it. Bobby Robicheaux had not been as lucky.

On the way over, in a halting, fumbling conversation between himself and Jim, Bobby recounted not only what Jim already knew—the fact that he was having tremendous difficulty re-acclimating to a world so far removed from the desert shooting galleries that were Iraq and Afghanistan that they might as well have been located on another planet entirely—but the most recent catalyst for Bobby's struggles: his closest friend from his platoon, Tom Dorsey, who lived twenty minutes away in Daly City and who worked with Bobby at the Port of Oakland (they were night-shift security guards) had, after having called in sick two nights earlier, calmly loaded his work-issued pistol, written three notes— one to his parents, one to his sister, and one to Bobby— sealed each of them carefully in matching envelopes, and shot himself through the mouth.

"They're all gone," Bobby said in the car, shaking his head from side to side. "Every one of them. There's nobody left."

"Except you," Jim answered, his hand on Bobby's shoulder. "You're still here, son. You're carrying the spirits of all those men in your heart."

We rode the rest of the way in silence, until Jim instructed me as to where the turn-off was for St. Anthony's Memorial Cemetery. We parked the car, locked the doors, climbed the fence as carefully as we could, and made our way through the darkness. Bobby lead us, moving so comfortably in the dark that it seemed like he was wearing night-vision goggles, and after a few minutes we arrived at Tom Dorsey's newly chiseled tomb. We couldn't make out what was written on the tomb, so I pulled out my iPhone and turned its brightness all the way up, so that it acted as a makeshift flashlight.

> Thomas Matthew Dorsey, 1987-2009
> Beloved Son and Brother and Patriot
> He Loved His Family and His Country

We stood there for the better part of five minutes, none of us speaking. Then Bobby knelt down to pull at some grass that had sprouted around the tomb's foundation. When he stood back up he placed the grass into his pocket, looked up at the stars for a moment, and then said to Jim,

"Will you say something for him? They had a funeral, but...maybe a little something more would be good, so he knows I'm here."

Jim moved to stand between us, taking each of our hands in his own. He bowed his head and closed his eyes. We followed suit.

"Dear Father, we pray tonight for the soul of Tom Dorsey. We pray that he finds solace with you, and that the pain he suffered on this earth is gone. We thank you for giving us the gift of Tom's life. Though we don't know why you felt it necessary to take him so early, we know that he is now beside you in Heaven, and will be an angel for the rest of his days. We pray all of this in your name, Father. Amen."

We stayed for a half an hour longer. Jim and I went for a walk so Bobby could be alone with Tom, and could mourn him privately for a time. As we moved through the grounds, the tombstones laid out in the kind of staggered fashion of an ancient Olympic obstacle course, we didn't speak, except when Jim, clearly not expecting a response, said,

"Some days I like this world a lot more than other days."

When we returned to Tom Dorsey's tomb, Bobby said to the two of us, "Let's go."

We walked back to the car. After Bobby gave me the address where he wanted to be dropped off, we turned the radio on as loud as we could, rolled down all of the windows, and sped through the deserted San Francisco streets listening to a series of early rock and roll classics from the 1950s. The voices of Gene Vincent and Elvis Presley and Little Richard seemed to sing passionately for the soul of Tom Dorsey, another gone son of a lost America.

Before Bobby stepped out of the car, he turned to Jim and said he'd call him tomorrow, and then turned to me, offered his hand, and, this time, meeting my eyes with his own.

"I hope I see you again, Patrick."

"Me too, Bobby," I answered. "Good luck to you."

We watched Bobby slowly make his way up the steps to his parents' house, the door opening when he was halfway up them. An older woman, presumably his mother, stepped out to welcome him in.

As we began the drive back to Jim's apartment, I said, "Jim, my father's wife sent me a letter my father had written before he died. He wanted to be buried with the silver medal that he won back in the 70s. Any chance you know where that medal might be?"

"With the Cloud Queen, probably."

"Who?" I asked.

"Penelope Ruth," he said, reaching over to turn the heater on in the car. "That's the woman you're looking for. She was like the Hippie Priestess of the Haight back in the day. Helped a lot of kids avoid the draft, gave money to guys like your father who didn't have any of their own, always seemed to have an extra room for guys coming back from the war who didn't know how to pick up the pieces of the lives they left behind. If she's still alive, I'm sure she's got your father's medal. She was like an unofficial guardian of anything valuable that people didn't want to put in the banks, or couldn't afford to."

"Why did they call her the Cloud Queen?" I asked.

"Rumor was that she grew the best pot in the city. It'd take you to the clouds after one puff." And after a pause, "That was what people told me," Jim said.

"But you had no first-hand knowledge of whether the pot was that good," I said, beginning to smile.

"Of course not," Jim said, winking.

"How old do you think she is at this point?"

"I don't know, two hundred?" he said, laughing, "She'd been around forever by the time I got out here, and that was back in the fifties. Anyway," he added, pulling a pen and small piece of paper out of this pocket, "here's where she used to live. But it's been years since I've seen her."

"Thanks for the tip, man," I said.

"Thanks for the ride-along tonight," he answered, putting his hand on my shoulder.

A few blocks later Jim said, "pull over here."

"My brother lives across the street," he said, pointing to a Victorian at the end of the darkened block. "He never sleeps. I think I'll drop in and watch the end of the game with him. Bring the car back whenever you're done with it. And if Penny is still alive, tell her I said hello. And that she owes me twenty bucks."

We shook hands and he added,

"Your father was a good man. I'm glad I knew him. Good luck, kid."

He stepped out of the car and headed up the block. For ten or fifteen seconds afterward I could hear his voice still softly whistling. At first I thought it was an old Irish shanty, its melody slow and unrecognizable, but after six or seven seconds I realized it was Louis Armstrong's "What a Wonderful World." It was a song I had grown up listening to with my grandparents on their record player, one more lovely relic of a Jazz Age that was never coming back.

Chapter 7
For Love of the Game

I turned the ignition, hit the AM dial and the car immediately filled back up with John Miller's laid-back, artless call: "It's the top of the ninth, one out. Zito on the mound. No runs, no hits, no walks, Jeter up to bat. Zito has pitched a wonder of a game."

There are few things in life as enjoyable for the American man as to be driving in a car late at night with a baseball game on the radio, his dashboard console a satellite-powered time machine, where the announcer's omniscient knowledge of the game can deliver a vanished (or at least vanishing) world back into the mobile landscape of his car. If America has produced only two original, homegrown cultural exports—baseball and jazz—then listening to either one of them is a subtle reminder that a nation is defined not by its politics nor its economic infrastructure nor even by its geographical topography, but by its pastimes.

"Strike three!" Miller exclaimed. "My goodness, he just hit 98 on the radar gun! And Jeter walks back to the dugout looking like he's seen a ghost."

"Well," Joe Morgan added. "He has, John. We all have. Barry Zito hasn't pitched like this since his Oakland days. And even then, he didn't have this kind of stuff."

"And we head now to the ninth inning. What's that old Vin Scully line? The crowd is seeing every pitch with its hearts now," Miller said, leading us into a commercial. Zito was three outs away from a perfect game.

I sat in the parked car across the street from Gemma's apartment building. I wanted to find out whether Zito could cap off this most extraordinary of accomplishments before knocking on her door. Indeed, for Barry Zito to somehow regain the Ace's form that fans and pundits alike were certain was gone forever, swallowed into that fickle and unforgiving abyss of athletic greatness, where men often woke up one morning to find the skills they had possessed just the day before had vanished in the night, never to be seen again, seemed to thrill me in a way I could not describe.

As I listened to Miller announce the first batter of the final inning, Hideki Matsui, an excellent hitter the Yankees had acquired from the Japanese league several years prior, I thought about the day and night now slowly drawing to a close. For the first time in as long as I could remember, possibly since I was Dorothy's age, when my bedroom walls were still covered with Magic Johnson posters and concert prints of Bruce Springsteen and Prince and Janet Jackson in her *Black Cat*-era bra and leather stirrups, I had become aware that the world was an outsized, sprawling Russian doll: a man cracked open his father's beating heart and found that entire landscapes had been hidden in its valves, irrigated by his iconoclastic blood, waiting like ancient Middle Eastern shrines and ruins to be discovered by some accidental archaeologist who didn't realize he was searching for something until he tripped over King Tut's gilded tomb.

"There's a grounder to second. Renteria makes the play! One out!" Miller shouted.

"And then there were two," Morgan added.

There were two old men crossing the intersection at the end of the block, both of them in matching trench coats and fedora hats, one with a walking stick that kept a riddling 4/4 rhythmic shuffle as he walked, the shorter one moving in a halting lilt that was clearly the result of a creaky set of knees. I watched them reach the other side and thought of the amazing good fortunes that had obviously been their lives, though I knew nothing at all about these men. The very fact that they were still here, though their bodies had aged like two WWII era submarines, out of date and no longer considered combat ready, was impressive enough. I imagined their night as it would unfold: there would be the Jewish deli where they would eat pastrami sandwiches, the television up above the counter playing highlights of the Giants-Yankees game, there would be the modest houses they would return to a little after 1am, their wives long having given up trying to wait up for them. While men like my father and Tom Dorsey had not—for reasons that were as different as those that the faithful and the agnostic use to justify their own sense of the world—lived to, in the words of Yeats, "comb gray hair," these men had won a kind of lottery, where the prize was not financial wealth but time itself. And with the radio on and the windows rolled down and these two men beginning to vanish from my line of sight, I realized that I actually wanted to live to be an old man. It was the only desirable scenario. Either you died young or you aged and dealt with the complications and difficulties.

"Now here is Rodriguez. Three-time AL MVP, only a handful of years away from becoming the game's all-time home run king. He's had a lot of success against Zito over the years, hitting .438 with six doubles and three home runs in

113

twenty-one at-bats. The crowd is on its feet, and it seems as if you can hear the cheering voices of the all-night fishermen out on the wharf and the shouts of the janitors washing the windows of the TransAmerica Pyramid rising up out of the fog."

Miller was getting romantic, a sportscaster-poet channeling his inner Kerouac to give us a sense of the moment. I couldn't blame him.

"And there's a hanging curve just off the corner. Ball. 1-1."

I sat in the car and looked up at the building, trying to pick out which window was Gemma's. Even at this late hour there were too many lights on, too many people probably still tuned into the miracle that appeared to be unfolding at the ballpark, and after strike number two I gave up and turned my attention back to the game.

"1-2 count. A-Rod signals for time and steps out of the box. The crowd boos as he taps the bat against each of his heels, retightens the straps of his batting gloves, and steps back into the box to face the man of the hour, Barry Zito."

A good three seconds went by in silence.

"Strike three! He got him on an eighty-three mile per hour change-up. Zito is one out away from pitching the first perfect game in Giants' history!"

"This is a special moment, John," Morgan, ever dignified and understated, chimed in, Lennon to Miller's McCartney.

I looked up again towards the tenth-floor windows, worried that I was pushing it by continuing to wait for the game to end. I had come to the crossroads every American man comes to more often than he would like to admit, that moment when he must decide, like a traveler in a Robert Frost poem, which of two paths to take: love or fandom?

And as any American man readily knows, there was never any real choice to begin with. The American Man is a sports fan first, a lover second. That's just the way things are. This fundamental truth separates us from them, good guys from bad, or, at least, us from the French.

"Now here's Posada. He's 1 for 3 on the night. Zito gets the signal from Molina."

"And here's a change-up that freezes Posada. Strike one. My goodness! We've seen that pitch at least twenty times tonight, and none of the Yankees have been able to figure it out," Miller marveled.

"Posada calls time. It looks like he's trying to disrupt Zito's rhythm."

"It's a little late for that John," Morgan said, in that deadpan, Jack Webb-like voice of his that often made him sound like a grizzled veteran on *Dragnet*.

"Strike two! Wow, a fastball that clocked in at 96 miles per hour. Posada again doesn't get the bat off of his shoulder. Listen to this crowd!" Miller exclaimed.

I couldn't tell if the roar that I could hear was entirely from the radio or whether the collective voices of nearly sixty thousand screaming and elated fans were strong enough to carry a couple of miles south to where I sat. Whatever the case, these were the moments you lived for as a sports fan, moments when you knew you were listening to something that might never happen again, and that the man performing the act of athletic greatness was almost certain to never again scale such heights. Tonight Barry Zito was like an aging Clark

Kent, surprised to find the cape still gave him powers he thought he had lost long ago.

"Here we go. Posada is ready. The crowd is on its feet. Zito goes into his wind-up…SWING AND A MISS! HE STRUCK HIM OUT! HE GOT JORGE POSADA SWINGING ON A HANGING CURVE! A PERFECT GAME FOR BARRY ZITO!"

Chapter 8
City Matadors

I didn't know if I should knock or ring the doorbell. It was 10:45, and though I knew Dorothy was probably sound asleep, I decided to knock as softly as I could.

Gemma opened the door wearing a San Francisco Giants t-shirt and nothing else. She held a glass of wine in her right hand.

"It was better on television," she said, nodding her head back towards the living room. "You should have come up."

"I couldn't risk the possibility that you weren't a sports fan," I said.

"I'm not a sports fan. I'm a baseball fan. There's a difference. Sports are something grown men play to work off their beer guts. Sports are something grown men watch to relive glory days most of them never had. Sports are too fast to even figure out what is even going on. What down is it? Where's the puck? What does deuce mean? Baseball is something else. Baseball is America as it was meant to be: no game clock, no violence, plenty of second chances, a place where you learn not to lose your confidence even though you have just struck out. Baseball is warm hot dogs, Sunday double-headers where you're sunburned by the sixth inning of the first game and your skin is peeling by the third inning of the second. Baseball is the only thing I used to do with my father. He taught me how to keep score. He taught me how to steal signs. He taught me how to put down a bunt by the time that I was six years old."

"What is this, *Bull Durham*?" I asked, smiling.

"No, I'm better looking than Kevin Costner was." She paused. "Are you going to come in or not?"

She sat like a yoga instructor on the sofa, her legs crossed beneath her like a peace sign composed of ridiculously perfect limbs, her hair falling onto her shirt like a windmill straight out of Don Quixote. I sat in the vintage chair across from her and tried not to fixate on those kneecaps of hers that looked like they were crying out for me to kiss them.

"I didn't think I'd be seeing you again. Especially after we had our *Casablanca* moment earlier this evening," she said.

Her skin was flushed, either from the effects of the wine she had been drinking or from the adrenaline rush the game had just provided.

"But I'm glad that you came back. I always wanted to stay in Casablanca with you, Rick," she said, this last sentence in an Ingrid Bergman-esque voice that would have made its original owner proud. All she was missing was the classic white hat, and a man far cooler and more world-weary than myself to say it to.

"Three hours without seeing you was about all that I could handle," I answered.

An hour later she was standing in the living room, her Giants t-shirt crumpled in my lap—she had thrown it towards me after I had, I still can't believe it, suggested that she let me see her naked—her body striking a goddess pose, arms make-believing she was holding a bow and arrow in her

118

hands, set to shoot a dart straight through the heart of an unsuspecting moon.

Goddamn, I said to myself. *Goddamn*.

"Now it's your turn," she said, stepping out of her pose and walking back to sit on the couch, folding her t-shirt a few times and then wrapping it around her forehead like a rock-and-roller's bandanna.

"And don't be shy," she added. "Bold is *sexy*."

If there is a God, I think it is safe to say he did men no favors in their attempts at being sexy. Where women have naturally shapely bodies, curves in all the right places, a set of hips that seem to know exactly where to go and how to sway at all times, the same cannot be said for men. We are, as John Updike once wrote, hyper-functional, a "delivery system" doomed to looking ridiculous on a dance floor. A woman dancer is, almost by definition, hot: all she has to do is lift her arms above her head and shake her ass and everyone's happy. A man, on the other hand, risks a level of ridiculousness the moment he begins to shake his hips that can be downright catastrophic in certain circumstances. Female strippers are almost invariably sexy; male strippers are comedy routines on *Saturday Night Live*.

I kicked off my right shoe and watched as it flew across the room and almost knocked over a lamp. I tried to smoothly slip out of my slacks and instead wound up almost falling over when my legs got tangled up in the fabric. In other words, Summer and Crystal and Mandy and Vivian and Venus and whoever else happened to be dancing down at the Condor Room across the street had nothing to worry about: I wasn't about to take anyone's job.

But I did my best, and Gemma kept smiling and trying to stifle her laughs so as not to wake Dorothy, and when I sent my shirt flying in her direction she caught it and stood up from the sofa and began to wave it like a matador in front of me.

I mock-charged and ducked my head into her belly, slipped down to my knees and started kissing her sex with an enthusiasm that I could not contain. She dropped the shirt and the last thing she said before slipping into a series of ridiculously alluring moans was,

"You're a terrible stripper but you put on one hell of a bullfight."

There is a difficulty in describing the act of sex that it seems only the Europeans have ever seemed to master. Most American writers either avoid the subject entirely, or, when they do decide to engage with the subject, do so in such a crass (gangster rap, Norman Mailer) or ridiculous (vampire films, Danielle Steele) manner that American literature seems to have a noticeable lack of meaningful sex scenes. If not for Henry Miller, we'd really be up a creek, and the truth is that he spent so much of his adult life outside of America that it's not really fair to claim him for ourselves.

All of this means that I'm not really sure how to describe the sex with Gemma other than to resort to words so overused they have been hollowed of any real meaning ("beautiful," "amazing," "transcendent," all words that are likewise used to describe an excellent sandwich or a Bruce Springsteen concert) or to employ tired pop culture similes— "it was like a cross between *Die Hard* and *The Bridges of Madison County*, only more exciting, and there was no

Nakatomi Tower," or, "imagine the feeling you get when listening to one of Eric Clapton's guitar solos from *Layla and Other Assorted Love Songs* while simultaneously watching Dr. J. dunk a basketball after taking off from the free throw line while also surfing the highest wave in the history of the Hawaiian North Shore. Only wearing a condom"—that still fail to truly convey just how wonderful making love to Gemma Lewis actually was.

Whatever the case, it lasted about forty-five minutes—thanks to the combination of a thick condom and the anxiety medication I had taken that morning—and afterwards we played an Emmylou Harris album on her record player.

"So tell me about tonight," she said. Her voice sounded like she had just smoked a carton of cigarettes. Quintessentially sexy, it was the Lauren Bacall voice without the nicotine scent or the yellow teeth.

"I found Jim O'Leary. A good man. One of those priests that you used to see in old Spencer Tracy movies. We talked about my parents for a couple of hours, watched the first several innings of the Giants game."

"Zito. Yeah, wow," she said.

"No kidding. He looked like Sandy Koufax out there," I said, sliding my left arm underneath her head, which she resettled on my chest. "Jim knew about the medal. He said that, at one point at least, this old woman who lived over on Telegraph Hill had it. Jim said she was an unofficial den mother for a lot of the college kids back in the 60s and early 70s, especially the ones with countercultural leanings or who had come from other countries. Rumor has it that she used to

121

hide the draft dodgers and help them make it to Canada. A local Harriet Tubman of the Vietnam War."

"Is she still alive?"

"He didn't know. Jim said she must have been pushing 80 decades back. But he said, 'you know how it is with these lasses, Patrick,' I said, trying to do my best Irish brogue. 'They live forever.' He loaned me his car. I figured I'd drive on out to Telegraph Hill tomorrow and see if she's still around."

"You want company?"

"Like a co-pilot?"

"Yes," she said, lifting her head off my chest to look at me. "Don't worry, I won't cramp your style."

The stereo needle started to drag. Gemma rose from the bed, her body soft in the silhouetted darkness of the room. I half expected her to be wearing wings, or to have a fishtail where her legs should have been.

She knelt down, her bare butt turned towards me like a fallen star, and rifled through the stacked collection of LPs she kept on the floor. After a minute or so she pulled one from its sleeve, set it gently down upon the turntable, and was back in bed by the time Springsteen's "Thunder Road" started filling the room with its optimism and its B-movie grandeur.

"Good choice," I said. She nodded towards her eastern wall, where a BRUCE SPRINGSTEEN FOR PRESIDENT bumper sticker hung, nestled in between an old concert playbill advertising Billie Holiday at the Cotton Club and an erotic still of Marilyn Monroe reclining on a red-sheeted bed, still the most beautiful *Playboy* spread the magazine had ever produced.

"I'm glad you came back," Gemma said, as Springsteen sang about screen doors slamming and the ghosts of burned-out Chevrolets speeding out of towns full of doomed and desperate losers.

Chapter 9
The Labyrinth of Telegraph Hill

I woke long before the sun the following morning and slipped out of bed to change the record that had hours earlier stopped playing. I put on Stevie Wonder's *Songs in the Key of Life*, still the greatest double-album of the pop music era, where Stevie single-handedly did what it took The Beatles four of them to do: shift so seamlessly between every imaginable popular musical style that Stevie seemed less like the second coming of Sam Cooke or Elvis Presley and more like a musical Da Vinci. *Songs in the Key of Life* is his Mona Lisa, a double LP possessed of so many beautiful songs I couldn't imagine anyone not including it on their desert-island short-list. This was something that my mother long ago told me, saying, while we sat on the beach, about a hundred yards from the fabled Huntington Beach Pier (which would collapse eight months later in a massive storm), "Stevie Wonder is the Patron Saint of American Music."

"Who's Stevie Wonder?" I asked, my child's eyes looking up at her in her wide-brimmed hat and her 1950s style sunglasses and the handmade beaded necklace that she had bought in a Haight Street vintage clothing store in the mid-70s.

"*Who's* Stevie Wonder?" she answered, smiling, playfully pinching my ear while straightening her hat with her other hand. "He's the only man whose music I played the entire time I was pregnant with you. *Songs in the Key of Life*, especially. I knew if you heard that often enough before you were born you would know everything that mattered in this world before you even got here: be good to women and animals, respect the environment, walk away from fights, stay away from drugs, and believe in a God who loves everyone equally."

"So Stevie Wonder is like Jesus?"

"Sweetie, Stevie Wonder *is* Jesus," she answered.

"Don't move, I want to get my camera," Gemma said a moment later, giggling, as I turned to see her sitting up in bed, her hands mock-framing the angles of my naked body, adding,

"I'm going to send this in to *Playgirl*. Baby needs a new pair of shoes."

I turned to face her and did a series of poses: The Heisman Trophy Pose, James Bond In Profile, his Walther PPK held beside his chiseled face.

"Oohh, you're a natural," she said, grabbing my cock as I got back into bed, sliding down to wrap her lips around it as I laid down, closed my eyes and tried to be entirely in the moment, even though an old joke my first literary agent had once told me entered my mind:

"People listen to Stevie Wonder when they're fucking, Neil Diamond when they're picking out their furniture, and Elvis Costello when they're signing their divorce papers."

A half an hour later Gemma and I were standing in her shower, after the two of us had checked in on Dorothy and found her sleeping so deeply I was for a moment concerned she had stopped breathing entirely.

"This is normal for her," Gemma had assured me. "She's like an Eskimo. She sleeps and her temperature drops.

Her heart rate too. It's crazy. She's a race car when she's awake and then a zombie the minute she hits the pillow."

"So what's the plan?" Gemma asked me as I ran my soap-filled hands along her shoulder blades, down the river of her spine and onto her beautifully full butt. Had she been an artist's model she would have been Renoir's favorite: curvy, fleshy, a full patch of pubic hair thick enough to have grown wildflowers inside, rather than one of Modigliani's pale, angular models, girls who always looked like they were stoned on downers, one bad break away from jumping out of their sixth floor windows.

I ran my hands along her sex, taking the little curls of hair into my fingers and pinching them gently.

"You like that?" she asked.

"Like it? I love everything that reminds me of the 1970s," I said, smiling.

"Get out of here," she said as she mock pushed me away.

"The plan?" I asked, getting back on topic, the water soothingly warm on our skin. "The plan is we put a full tank of gas in the car, find a good radio station to listen to, roll down the windows and go find Penny Ruth."

"You've seen *The Blues Brothers* too many times."

"There's no such thing," I said, daubing shampoo onto my palms.

I sat at the dining room table while Gemma made a breakfast fit for the gods of Mt. Olympus, had those gods gone vegan—all-wheat waffles, organic honey, freshly-squeezed orange juice, french toast, no butter, ground cinnamon, and enough strawberries to have fed the three hundred thousand plus who raided Yasgur's farm all those years ago.

Dorothy walked in just as Gemma was setting down the food-filled plates.

"It's one of my bionic powers, Patrick," Dorothy sleepily said. "I can smell food from up to ten miles away."

"What are the others?" I asked, playfully tussling her hair.

"I know whenever someone is about to take a trip without me."

"You want to come, sweetheart? We'd love to have you along."

"I'm just kidding you, Patrick," she answered. "It's Comic Con today. I'm going with a friend. Her mom is driving us. She's going as Catwoman. My friend is going as Princess Leia. I'm going as Luke Skywalker."

"You have a light saber?" I asked.

"Are the Beatles the greatest rock band who ever lived? Of course I have a light saber, Patrick. A blue one, too, so don't worry. I've resisted the Sith forces just like I've resisted the forces of alcohol and drugs."

We sat around the table and, for the second time in twenty-four hours, had a meal that, in spite of the fact I was eager to get on the road and try to find the mysterious Penny Ruth, I did not want to end. For most of my life the meals I had with others always felt as if someone was missing: my father, usually, when he was off on walkabout, leaving my mother and me to eat alone, though the two of us happily devoured television shows that we treated as interactive, audience-participation exercises straight out of Restoration

Drama: *Magnum, P.I., Happy Days, The A-Team, The Dukes of Hazard, Matt Houston, Crazy Like a Fox, Cheers, Quantum Leap.*

And there was nothing like listening to Dorothy once she'd got her sea legs under her, riffing like a lightweight, adolescent shock jock or cultural pundit on just about any subject imaginable:

"Fleetwood Mac *was* Lindsay Buckingham...I'm going to marry Robert Redford...Bill Clinton was a great President...I never liked DC Comics...Except Wonder Woman..."

In many ways, sitting at a breakfast table with Dorothy Lewis was something you felt she could have charged admission for, a performance where her audience (of two) marveled at the breadth of her knowledge, her love of popular culture, her ability to synthesize and see connections between seemingly disparate strands of information in ways that would have impressed NASA's scientists or *Rolling Stone*'s editorial board. It was clear she was going to spend her life being the smartest person in any room she walked into, but it was equally clear that she had such an innate goodness—no doubt aided by her older sister's gentle, equally-spirited and good-hearted hand—that she would not grow into the bully that so many people blessed with the type of brains she possessed ultimately became.

"Luke Skywalker wasn't half the Jedi you already are, kiddo," I said.

Dorothy smiled, grabbed a waffle and sprinted back into her room to change.

A few minutes later the doorbell rang. Three seconds later Dorothy had sprinted from her room to the table, had somehow kissed both Gemma and me on the cheeks, grabbed her light saber from her room and was saying goodbye as she headed out the door, Gemma and I having caught only the briefest glimpse of a pint-sized Princess Leia with crow-black hair in the doorway.

"Forget a Jedi Knight," I said, "She should have gone as the Flash."

"That's nothing," Gemma answered. "You should see how fast she makes it out of school. Two seconds after the bell rings she is on the sidewalk in front of school, tapping me on the shoulder, ready to be on the BART heading home."

"Speaking of which. We don't need to move quite as quickly, but we should be getting ready to hit the road ourselves."

"Penelope awaits," Gemma said. "I haven't been on a real quest since the time my girlfriends and I went looking for that Chippendale's club on the day we turned eighteen."

"Did you find what you were looking for?" I asked.

"A true knight never reveals her secrets," she said, shaking her head coyly. "But I will say since then I've always had a quite a thing for men in bow ties."

"I'll have to check my suitcase," I said.

The address that Father Jim had given me— handwritten in something that, on first glance, looked to be ancient Sanskrit or, at the very least, early Christian Aramaic that made me wonder if I needed a scholar of classical, pre-modern literature to translate what exactly the good father had written down—was 75 Paris Street. As coda, he had mentioned that there used to be a statue of the Lady of the Lake at the end of the street.

All morning I had been thinking about why it was that my parents—and now I— had bonded so immediately with a Jesuit priest who believed Eden was not a mythic place akin to Arthur's Avalon or the Valhalla of the pagan Vikings, but an actual landscape where two people had been foreclosed on for violating the terms of their lease. This brief note reminded me: he was a romantic, a nostalgic who saw contemporary life as being a place that consistently repatriated, if not downright devoured, its magic. For him, Catholicism did the work that Walt Whitman's poetry and Dylan's music did for me: it treated America as a surgeon does a cancerous but savable lung: he takes a scalpel to the skin and systematically removes the infected areas, and then he sews it back up as best he can. In that way, post-op, we tell ourselves to believe that if one only went far back enough, into some vast and formerly inaccessible past where it never rained and there was always enough food to go around, we would find a place where life made sense, and where we spoke the language.

But of course, the thing with nostalgia is that it is like the horizon. It keeps moving farther back the closer you think you are getting to it. In this way, I knew that twenty years from that afternoon I would be lamenting what America had been at that very moment, the morning after Barry Zito had pitched a perfect game, the morning after Bobby Robicheaux had said goodbye to his closest friend, the morning after I had fallen in love with Gemma Lewis, the morning after I realized I was close to relocating my father's medal.

Five minutes later Gemma emerged from her bedroom wearing a floor-length white skirt, a blue cotton blouse and black boots. She looked stunning.

"Do I look all right?" she asked, turning her toes slightly inward and biting her bottom lip like a high school girl getting ready for her first date.

"All right?" I responded. "Just tell me the name of which bank you want me to rob."

She laughed and tried to divert my attention from a deepening blush by walking towards the door and asking,

"Are you ready?"

"I was thirty seconds ago," I said. "Now all I want to do is take you back to bed."

She turned and kissed me, wrapping her arms around my neck.

"Are you this charming for all the girls?"

When we got down to the car she stopped a few feet from it, admiring it from the sidewalk as if it were the skeleton of an ancient saber-toothed tiger in a natural history museum.

"My God. It's the Batmobile."

"No kidding," I answered. "I'm fairly certain there are machine guns hidden in the headlights, and both front seats can be converted into jet packs if we hit some really awful traffic."

"Well, should we hit the road?" I asked, after another moment.

"Absolutely," Gemma answered.

After a few blocks through typically crowded weekend streets, we began to roll through the boulevards whose buildings were housing this year's Comic Con Festival.

After years of being held in the Gaslamp District of coastal San Diego, the three-day extravaganza had come north, bringing with it several thousand of the billion or so comic book lovers who had seen to it that the modern comic book film was consistently the most popular and profitable of Hollywood products. By the second block we had seen a handful of storm troopers, two Jokers, one Catwoman, one Superman, and what may or may not have been a transvestite hooker who had gotten into the spirit of the day by wearing the leave-nothing-to-the-imagination unitard of Aeon Flux. While on Hollywood Boulevard this type of scene would have been a normal Tuesday afternoon, business as usual in a town where you routinely found yourself sitting next to people in full studio costume as you ate a burger at a local Hollywood diner, in the relatively classy cultural environs of San Francisco, it seemed like Mardi Gras had found its way west.

"Oh my God, I want her body," Gemma said, nodding in the direction of a thirty-ish stunner dressed as Wonder Woman, her breasts so impressively full they could have saved a plane-full of crash survivors from drowning in the ocean, her thigh-high boots wrapped tightly around a set of legs that, had this been a Humphrey Bogart film, he would have called a "perfect set of gams."

I had played this game before.

"She's got nothing on you." I said, placing my hand on her thigh.

"Please," Gemma said. "You don't need to do that with me. I'd so get naked with her," she said, turning back to marvel as Wonder Woman made her way across the crosswalk.

"Hold on," I said, "I'm turning the car around."

Gemma laughed.

"What is it with you guys? The thought of two girls together always turns guys on."

"I don't see what's so mysterious about it," I answered, gently pushing down on the accelerator as the light turned green. "The only thing better than one naked woman is two naked women. Especially if they let you watch."

"Men are so weird."

"Weird? Brilliant, was more what I was thinking."

Gemma leaned over to kiss me on the cheek.

"Ok, sweetie. I promise you that if I ever decide to have sex with Wonder Woman, I'll make sure to let you watch."

"And take photographs," I added.

"And take photographs."

"Thank you. Was that so hard? We don't ask for much."

We passed the TransAmerica Pyramid, that architectural celebration of American capitalism that had effectively annihilated one of the oldest and most treasured bohemian haunts in all of America. We were a few minutes away from the bottom of Telegraph Hill.

Telegraph Hill was one of the fabled Seven Hills of San Francisco. It was a lovely area, especially so at night, where one had panoramic views of the city lights in the same way the Parisian nightscape was never prettier than when it was glimpsed from the rooftop viewing platform of the Arc de Triomphe. It should not have surprised me that this was where Penny Ruth lived.

I put the car in neutral at the top of the hill, and stepped out to look at the respective addresses of the houses, which seemed to be almost entirely hidden in a street-wide game of Guess-Who-Lives-Here? If San Francisco was, in fact, a mailman's nightmare, a postal Dante's Inferno where those who had likely sinned in some previous life were sent to this labyrinth of vanished addresses to atone, then Telegraph Hill was its final circle, boasting a series of streets where one could never be lost because one was not aware of where he was in the first place.

"Wait here. I'll take a look around," I said, leaving the keys in the ignition.

The houses were like installations constructed by an ambitious contemporary artist who had been given an unlimited budget by the Museum of Modern Art. Though the majority of Americans thought San Francisco strange because of its countercultural history, its tolerance of bikers, hippies, draft dodgers and flamboyant gays, the truth was that the only genuinely strange component of the city was that it often seemed to be the emptiest big city in America: a place where 1 million people somehow never emerged from the homes they were said to inhabit.

In other words, I couldn't find the fucking house and there was no one around that I could ask for directions. I got back into the car.

"Jesus," I said. "Where the hell is everybody?" I asked, laughing, trying to figure out what our next step would be.

"You guys lost?" a voice said, suddenly filling the car with its weathered gravity.

We both turned to see a man standing next to my window, who apparently had either appeared out of thin air, or was an ex-CIA spook with a gift for sneaking up on people only rivaled by mimes and ninjas.

He looked like Captain Ahab, if Captain Ahab had spent his life fixing cars instead of sailing ships, his tanned face, darkened with smudges of black that looked as if he had been preparing for a football game that was called off at the last moment, his ripped, dirtied denim shirt and jeans so lived-in, so authentic that it made James Dean and Jack Kerouac and *Streetcar*-era Marlon Brando look like phonies by comparison. He looked like the kind of guy who John the Baptist should have hired as a bodyguard when things started getting hot back in Palestine.

"Yes, we're looking for 75 Paris Street," I said.

He looked off in the direction of the Golden Gate Bridge, which was barely visible from this particular location, and then back at us for a moment. It was as if he were sizing us up, gauging our goodness and our honesty the way an investigating officer might, or St. Peter might at the big roll call. After a good thirty seconds he answered,

"Penny's place?"

"Yes," Gemma said from over my shoulder. "Do you know where we can find her?"

After another extended pause, this one about fifteen seconds long, which I took as a sign he was warming to us, he said,

"She lives one street over. You're on River Street. Paris is the next one down."

"Thank you," I said.

"But she ain't there," he added.

Over the next few minutes the man told us that Penelope, now too old to live on her own, had left her house to her daughter and was living with her granddaughter in a small town outside of Portland.

"But her mind's still as sharp as it ever was. If she knew your father, she'll still remember him," he assured us.

A few minutes later we were driving back towards the apartment. Gemma leaned over and turned the radio on once we had turned the corner. She settled on an old Peter Gabriel song, "Washing of the Water." If there was a heaven, I'd always hoped that a Peter Gabriel ballad was playing on the stereo when we got up to the gates. Something off of *So* or *Us*. One of those stately five-minute numbers where it sounded like Pete was atoning for the sins of an entire generation of lost souls, all of them, to my mind, deserving of a second chance to right the wrongs they had committed.

"I love his music," I said.

"I figured you would," Gemma answered, putting her hand on my shoulder.

Chapter 10
Going to Meet the Cloud Queen

You had forgotten that was what the country used to look like. You had forgotten that once there were fields that stretched so far into the distance that the few roads there were seemed like aberrations, glitches in God's prototype that his son would fix upon his imminent return. For a man like me, someone for whom the closest he had ever come to being Robert Frost was on an occasional morning bike ride through Crystal Cove State Beach, doing seventy-five miles an hour on an open straightaway like Highway 617, where the trees outnumbered the cars twenty-five to one, and where the sky was the kind of blue that the smog simply never allows it to approach in Los Angeles, felt less like a fuel-injected sprint through the Pacific Northwest and more like outright time travel, as if I were driving back into the beating heart of an America that hadn't existed in any meaningful sense since my grandmother was a child in rural Ohio.

I had no interest in turning on the radio, and felt no need to even sing to myself as I watched the miles tick past. It was as if the only appropriate state of being for such natural beauty was the silence usually reserved for church, and though I knew I could never live in a place quite as off the beaten path as this, I also understood why so many left behind the cities to return to the small town, or, in the case of this stretch of road, no-town way of life of places like rustic Oregon. Beyond my car windows was a landscape I had only previously seen in the country paintings of Edward Hopper, those magic realist tone poems to an earth beatified and haunted in equal measure.

After an hour's drive from Portland I arrived in Silverton and slowed down to appreciate the classic Main Street structures and the red and yellow candy-cane signifiers rising from the windows of the local stores. I read the hand-painted signs advertising the blackberry festival that was now only days away. I could actually feel my heart rate begin to decrease and my breath slow down to a pace that only yoga mystics and underwater scuba divers could truly understand. By the time I saw the turn-off for the Ruth farm and began to follow the winding gravel road into a thicket of woods that looked like they had been planted by the Grimm Brothers, I felt something I don't think I had ever felt before, not peace exactly, but instead a sense that I had somehow come upon a place where it was possible to make time stand still. I was a City Merlin come to the Pacific Northwest, prepared to use his sudden powers not to overthrow a kingdom, but instead to make sure the people that he loved would have their desires met.

It wasn't so much a farm as it was a small house in the middle of an enormous stretch of land, a cottage like the ones you see a lot in Western Europe. As I pulled into the dirt driveway and parked, a young woman—Penny's granddaughter, I assumed—stepped out from behind the creaking screen door and watched, clearly surprised to have a visitor so early in the morning.

"Hello," I said, walking towards the porch, aware that it was almost impossible not to look like a traveling encyclopedia salesman or an over-eager Jehovah's Witness when walking up to meet the woman of a house whom you have never met.

"My name is Patrick Karimi. I'm looking for Penelope Ruth. Is she around?"

"She's at church," the woman said, a lightness in her voice that made it sound as if she was always on the verge of singing. "What is this is regarding?"

"My father…" I began, aware that what I was about to say was going to sound ridiculous, unless, of course, the granddaughter was aware that her grandmother had been something of an unofficial fairy godmother for an entire city in an earlier era of her life.

"…Well, he asked Mrs. Ruth to hold onto something that was very important to him, and I've come to retrieve it."

She nodded, looked out past me to my car, a gleaming blue Accord with Portland plates and a conspicuous AVIS sticker in the windshield.

"What is it?" she asked.

"A silver medal."

"Like an Olympic medal?" she asked, intrigued, her eyes conveying the fact that her grandmother was clearly still a constant revelation, not an enigma so much as a mansion with many as yet unopened rooms. Her blue dress swirled a little bit in the breeze.

"Yes. A soccer medal," I answered. "My father was on the Iranian National Team back in the early 70s. The goalie. Your grandmother—Penelope is your grandmother?—held onto it for him when he didn't think he wanted it anymore. But," I added, after a pause. "My father died last week, and his wishes were that it be buried with him."

139

"Come on inside," the woman, whose name I still did not know, said. "Mass should be out by now. They'll be dropping her off any minute. I'll make us some tea."

If I had taken the time to think about what the inside of the house would look like, it would have looked exactly as it actually did: old wood floors, cast iron fixtures, a cat sleeping on an empty, overstuffed, slightly aged chair, two dogs playing in the field beyond the window that opened out onto a series of orchards, a chicken coop, and a llama pen. Okay, the llama pen was not something I would have expected, and I said as much.

"Are those llamas?" I asked.

"You make it sound like they're unicorns," she said, laughing. "I'm Alyssa, by the way."

"Patrick," I said.

"Yeah, you mentioned that. I thought you were coming to sell me a slice of Heaven until I saw it was a rental car."

"No, if I'd been selling you a piece of Heaven I would have arrived on a bicycle. God doesn't do company cars," I joked.

Over the next half an hour I filled Alyssa in on who my father was, who her grandmother had been in San Francisco, and how I had tracked her down. It was only at the mention of Father Jim O'Leary that she caught her breath a bit.

"You know him?" I asked.

"No, we've never met. But grandma has pictures of the two of them. Jim was close with my father. They met in Vietnam. Jim was a unit priest over there."

"I didn't know that."

"When Dad died it was Jim who delivered the letter to my mother. Grandma always said Jim O'Leary was one of the kindest men she ever met."

"I'd second that," I said.

A moment later we heard a car in the driveway, the opening and closing of doors, a bit of laughter. As the two of us stood to go to the door, I caught sight of a photograph on the wall that must have been Alyssa's father, dressed in his fatigues, a rifle in hand, surrounded by a quartet of similarly outfitted comrades.

Penelope Ruth looked every bit as old as I thought she would and yet somehow divorced from time completely. With her thin mane of white hair, her wooden cane, and her blue dress that went all the way down to the floor, she had the aura of a female Galahad, a Grail Queen whose weakness was not a result of wounds sustained in battle but from the effects of a life spent simply enduring, watching entire generations grow up, grow old, and die. It was clear she was a kind of guardian, a figurative Lady of the Lake, only what she had dominion over was not a mystical body of water but instead the histories of a generation of men who had not survived to reclaim what they had not been able to let go. Aided by Alyssa, Penelope climbed the steps with the dignity that Hemingway movingly wrote about in "A Clean, Well-Lighted Place," as the solitary old man, a little drunk on wine and melancholy, walks ably into the darkness of an empty Spanish street.

"You're Hassan's son," she said, without the least touch of surprise. "You have his eyes. His hair too," she said, touching my shoulder gently. "Come on inside. I have something that belongs to him."

I could talk about the rest of the day I spent with Alyssa and Penelope Ruth. I could talk about the walk the three of us took into the woods where we saw a solitary elk drinking from a creek, its horns as whirled and as sturdy as the infrastructure of an old Coney Island rollercoaster. I could talk about the stories Penny told us about my father, about how he was the best violin player that she ever saw—I didn't know he had played at all—and that it was on the night he tore his ankle up in an intramural soccer game, the same night when he also found out a political activist friend of his back home had disappeared under mysterious circumstances, that he threw his medal into the trash and said he didn't want it anymore. I could talk about how she said she didn't try to talk him out of it, but instead waited until he left and then pulled it out of the bin, cleaned it with a rag, and then stored it away for safekeeping, or about how amazed I was at Penelope's ability to walk so deeply into a forest where the terrain was rigorously uneven. I could even talk about the fact that, as I was getting into my car to leave, Alyssa hugged me warmly and Penelope kissed me on the cheek, ran her hand through my hair and said, "Don't cut it. Don't ever cut it. A man's strength is in his hair," but I'm not sure I could do any of it justice. Some things are best left to silence, I guess.

I was back at my hotel in Portland by eleven o'clock that night, just in time to catch the lead story on Sportscenter: LeBron James had just scored 57 points in Game 1 of the NBA Finals. After a short phone call to Gemma, I was in bed a few minutes after midnight.

Chapter 11
All Roads Lead Back to Persepolis

I've always loved airports. While train stations are romantic in the same way that black and white films are romantic, both of them capturing some vestige of a vanished world that seems, upon reflection, more beautiful and mythic than our own, airports make me feel like I've stepped into the future, as if they are the ultra-modern gateway to a world where gravity itself is a relic of the past. It's why I arrived at Oakland International several hours early, found a seat in a quiet terminal, and fell asleep almost immediately.

It was not a smile but a certainty. A faith in magic necessitated by exile. Years later, upon reading The Great Gatsby, it dawned on me that my father's smile reflected not how you most wanted to be seen, but what remained of you in the absence of his own sight. No desire for clarity; the veil was beauty, mystery, shadow. The poetry of the felt, the dreamed, was what he called forth in these moments, from some depth that was more reservoir than sensory. Though this was certainly not the first time I had received his gift (the first was, most likely, the day I was born, when my mother, protected from an early winter storm by her hospital room on the third floor, broke what must have been a San Francisco General record for speed in the delivery room), it was the first time I had been aware of its power. It registered to me as something not unlike madness, though it was the type of madness a singer has at his most breathtaking, perhaps when he is, in the midst of a dirge of undeniable beauty, swept beyond the mathematical world of octaves and melodies and arrives, however fleetingly, in the sun-capped furrows of a mountainside belonging neither to this world nor to any other, except to that planet which houses the infinity of imagined dreamscapes the singer carries within himself, as a physicist does Einstein's theories of relativity.

This recognition was short-lived. Moments later he was gone, swept up by the oceans (it was high-tide, it was Newport Beach, it was stupid for us to be out there) that he had insisted he knew so well. However, possessed of the blind faith unique to him of my little league experience and kindergarten education, I did not take into account the fact that my father knew as much about this land of oceans he had immigrated to, as I did about the secrets of love. And so I was left to await his rising, which did not come for a solid three minutes (I had my Mickey Mouse watch to thank for such exactitude), some hundred yards off the jetty, and with not another human being (outside of myself) in sight.

It was a long swim.

It was one of those swims that seem to speak to the entire process of man's evolution, where each stroke was summoned up out of an endless well of time and history that, through its obvious endurance, supersedes all religion in its manifestation. Christ was not a gleam in young Mary's eye (nor Joseph's, to be perfectly honest) when my father's freestyle abilities were first being honed by some gallant caveman who had, at the close of a thousand years of winter, awoken one morning to find his front yard curling in blue foam, and his admittedly primitive lawn furniture being swept away by a thoughtless sea. To my father's credit, he embraced his place in history (and, certainly, he was aware that my mother was going to be seriously pissed if I came home without him), and swam like a man being chased by a family of sharks.

His staggering up onto the rocks furthered this allusion to Darwin's theory in action, as his breathless grunts, his bloodied forehead, his shorn clothes, and his wild eyes all spoke to his impromptu role in the Survival of Man.

I stood there, arms at my sides, mouth frozen into something resembling terror, and let him walk to me. (Fear, ever the iconoclast, evidently did not believe in admitting the need for a father's hug, no matter the circumstances). Instead of an impassioned embrace, something out of the Clint Eastwood school of, it's-alright-for-one-man-to-hug-another-because-we-just-lived-through-the-apocalypse-and-there's-nobody-around-to-see-us, he merely rested a hand on my shoulder, leaned towards me, and smiled.

Fucking smiled, and said: "So, do you want to stay and fish some more? Or do you want to go home?" as casually as a man who had spent the hours of the late afternoon casting bait from some idyllic lakeside embankment, the warmth of a fire and a woman's love behind him, instead of caught in our current predicament, which seemed, if nothing else, to resemble some forgotten Melville story, perhaps one that centered on Ahab's younger, and physically healthier, brother.

Not knowing what to say, but realizing this was probably a moment he saw as illuminating whether his young son had the ability to shrug off a rather violent confrontation with mortality and re-assume a mantle of relaxed bravado, I haltingly answered, "Let's stay a while longer."

I woke to the sound of a young boy and girl giggling as they skipped down the aisle where I sat, their mother fumbling with their assembled luggage, calling out to them to slow down with the defeated tone of a good woman who knows the chips have simply been stacked against her.

Ah, the last fishing trip! Though it had taken place nearly thirty years ago, it was an experience that I often thought about, both because the sea had looked uncommonly beautiful, the sun's setting light spreading out across the tides like a Chinese fan, the waves curling like so many calligraphic letters from a foreign alphabet, and because it seemed to be one of, to me, the most action-packed of my father's long line of near-death experiences.

But as I gradually adjusted to the bustle of an airport that was rapidly filling up with people, it occurred to me that I had overlooked the most important component of that ill-fated fishing trip: we had gone out at high tide because my father wanted me to see the world for what it was, a place whose pleasures always came with a requisite modicum of danger. In other words, anything worth doing was something you might not make it back from.

To be entirely truthful, it was not a motto I had taken to heart. In fact, I had spent the majority of my adult life avoiding dangerous situations—I stayed away from the motorcycles my father loved to ride, and I never learned to surf because I was scared of being caught beneath the tides—and it had only been during that past week, when my father had reached up from the dreaming sea of death to ask me to fulfill his last request, that I had found myself embracing the free-spirited ethos that he possessed on a daily basis. Perhaps that had been my greatest failing as a son: I had not looked at my father through the right kind of eyes. He did not want to be seen as a mythic figure, the last of a dying breed, but as a man who most embraced the short amount of time that God has afforded him. Or maybe I was simply being sentimental. Either way, by the time the flight attendant had announced Flight 235 was now boarding, I knew that there was something other than the silver medal that I had tucked into my carry-on luggage that I owed my father's memory: I had spent my twenties proving to myself all the ways in which I was nothing like him, but now, nearly halfway into my thirties, it was time to exhibit the ways in which I was exactly like him. Which meant that, upon returning from Iran, I would go back to San Francisco, take a cab to Gemma's apartment, and tell her that I was in love with her. San Francisco would once again be the city that would bring out the secret romantic in a Karimi man.

Sitting in the window seat that looked out onto the plane's eastern wing, I felt like my life was, in some fundamental way, beginning again, and I spent the hours in the air reading Michael Ondaatje's superb novel *Divisadero*, excited to be a day away from seeing the country of my father's birth.

Regardless of which airport you find yourself in, and no matter in what part of the world that airport is located within, the scene in airport terminals is always the same: loved ones stand smiling expectantly, valets hold signs written in the local language that announce themselves to passengers they have been hired to pick up, and airport personnel move swiftly through the assembled throngs, pushing old women in wheelchairs to their desired gates, carrying misplaced luggage to the appropriate conveyor belts.

And once in a while, a father thought to have died in his sleep stands holding a handwritten placard with the name Patrick Karimi on it.

Goddamn.

I should not, of course, have been surprised to see him standing there, his hair gone fully gray but still as thick as it was when I last saw him, his navy blue wool pants and white collared shirt manifesting a fashion sense he hadn't always shown, his smile something I had come to recognize as a product of his good-natured hubris: he never understood why sometimes those around him didn't always find the same things as funny as he did.

But I had never been one of those people. I was already laughing as I walked towards him, his arms stretched wide, his smile broad enough to make it seem like he had just won an Academy Award.

We shook hands and embraced.

"Good to see you, Patrick," my father said. "You made it."

"I have to say, Dad, you're the best looking dead man I've ever seen."

He nodded and laughed some more.

"I figured you knew when I had Nazim tell you that I died in my sleep that I wasn't really dead. But it was the only way I could be sure you would come."

"You didn't think a simple phone call would do?"

"No way. A simple phone call wouldn't get me on a plane. Nothing short of death is going to inspire a man to spend twenty-five hours on a series of jets."

In the speeding taxicab—albeit one without a braying goat strapped to the roof—my father recounted the motive behind the retrieval of his medal.

"Oh, that thing means nothing to me. Hell, I would have let it stay with Penny except that there's this orphanage I want to start. All these kids, you know? So many wars, parents dead or disappeared. And I can sell it for 25,000 dollars. Not rials. *Dollars*," my father emphasized. "Some of these sports collectors are just out of hand. I could get something out of the bottom of a Cracker Jack box that would look almost exactly the same as the medal. Who needs it? Anyway. That money is going to help get the place built."

After I nodded my head in agreement—what else could I do?—he paused for another few seconds and then said, "And I wanted to see you, Patrick. It's been ten years."

Rather than going to my hotel, the two of us instead drove out to Persepolis—"there's a place I've been wanting to take you since you were a little kid, Patrick," my father said—that ruined City of the Kings that had remained a source of myth for me since I was a boy. I had so often imagined my father taking picnics in its crumbling amphitheater, of him taking evening walks alongside the River Kir, of him leaning against the pillars of the Gate of Nations as a light rain was beginning to fall, that I felt like it was a place I had actually been to before. Thus, it seemed fitting that, only minutes after realizing my father was, in fact, very much alive, it would be to Persepolis, site of stone bas reliefs as richly beautiful as anything on earth, home of palaces that had once been sites of revelry which made even the most decadent scenes of Marie Antoinette's Versailles seem downright tame by comparison, that we decided to go.

The air hummed with the energy of a landscape that had once been home to gods and kings. In my imagination, Persepolis and my father were connected the same way that Odysseus was with Ithaca, Aeneas with Rome. In other words, it had been worth the week of thinking that my father was dead to have that one evening with him in one of the oldest places on earth, a desert Atlantis where two men were able to remind themselves that they still loved one another, and that they had, in fact, never really been apart.

Even more importantly: there was a soccer game going on.

There were ten of them, all boys, between the ages of nine and twelve, many of them barefoot, others wearing Adidas cleats of the kind that I had last worn in AYSO soccer leagues during elementary school. Some wore simple t-shirts, others wore replica jerseys with the names and numbers of their favorite players emblazoned on the back. As was to be expected, none of the players seemed particularly reverent—if they were even aware at all—of the genuine grandeur that their impromptu field had possessed. As was the case anywhere in the world, children were not only oblivious of history, but outside of it. To them, Persepolis was an ideal place to play a game of soccer because there was plenty of space to run, because the stone pillars made for perfect goalposts, and because, most importantly of all, there weren't any parents around to call them in to dinner. Or put another way: empires rise and fall, but playgrounds are forever.

"These kids are here almost every afternoon and evening," my father said, nodding his head in the direction of the goalie, a bushy-haired boy with spindly legs and feet that appeared to be the size of dual battleship destroyers, who had just waved hello to him.

"Baseball may be the American pastime," my father said. "But soccer is our national religion. A team wins a World Series in America and everyone celebrates for three hours, goes out to a bar and has a few beers, maybe burns a police car or two in hopes of starting a mini-riot. Iran wins a national game and the President declares a holiday, everyone stays home from school, and parades occur all across the country. American sports fans have always been amateurs," he said, smiling.

As I was about to respond, two kids who looked like siblings, the older one just beginning to show the outline of a mustache beneath his deeply tanned nose, came running over.

After a few moments of conversing in Farsi, my father turned to me and said:

"They want us to play. What do you think?"

"I think I've been sitting on an airplane for the last twenty-four hours, and it'd feel good to run around a little bit," I answered.

I hadn't played since college, back when on Tuesday nights I'd play mid-fielder in co-ed intramural games where the majority of one's enjoyment came not from running up and down the field, but from watching some of the beautiful Santa Barbara girls run up and down the field beside you. But such an extended layoff didn't really matter. You never forget how to play a sport. If, indeed, you don't slip back into it quite as smoothly as you do when it comes to riding a bike for the first time in years, the truth is that after two or three minutes of passing the ball back and forth, dribbling it down the pitch and kicking it to an open teammate—in this case, those open teammates were mostly kids who were still young enough to wear braces or to have been born too late to have any idea of who men like Pele or Diego Maradona actually were—you felt as if it had only been a day or two since the last time that you wore a pair of cleats.

My father, even in dress shoes that looked like they cost him more than what my plane ticket had cost, had clearly not lost much since his own prime. He wowed the kids with his fancy dribbling, at times so much so that the game stopped, and they would huddle around him to watch him quickly bounce the ball on his toes ten, twenty, thirty times without the ball ever touching the ground, then bouncing it off his thighs, his chest, the top of his head with a seamlessness and a relaxed, good-natured showmanship that had always come naturally to him. When the game would resume again, he would still have the smile on his face as he joyously called out encouragements and instructions to the kids on his team *and* the kids on the other side, as he clapped when someone made a particularly impressive goal, as he laughed when someone made a mistake by accidentally kicking the ball out of bounds (which, in this case, was a rather amorphous delineation. If the ball went out past the Apadana Staircase, you had clearly gone too far).

It reminded me of the times when I was a kid and my father would walk out across the street to the park where I was playing with my friends, and happily join the game of full-court basketball we had going on. Every time I would score a basket he would always wink in my direction, as if to remind me that, yes, it's fun being out here with all of these kids, but *you* are my son, the only one that I am really rooting for. There were times in those games that we'd also have to stop because my father would suddenly be inspired to use the basketball as a stand-in for a soccer ball, doing the exact same type of tricks he had just shown off moments earlier on the desert pitch, wowing my friends to such a degree that rumors, which being a typical kid, I did nothing to quench, that he had in fact been a professional player for years and years, until his home country kicked him out for just being too damned good.

In other words, that game of soccer beside the ruins of Persepolis was more than merely déjà vu, it was outright time travel. I had flown ten thousand miles to land in the country of my own childhood, a place where the games seemed to go on forever, and where everyone seemed happy at the outcome of the contests, no matter what the final score. My father, in fact, had seemingly re-created some of the happiest moments of his own fatherhood experiences by returning to the land where he was born. It was a wonderful thing to see.

We played for the better part of an hour. The kids seemed somewhat in awe of me—I was Hassan Karimi's son—and this seemed to immediately give me a sense of stature in their eyes. It was not until a car pulled up and a father stepped out to greet my father, a friend of his from town (and a father to one of the boys in the game), that the game began to wind down. One by one, in twos and threes, boys were picked up by parents, or got on their bicycles to ride on into an adolescence that they did not know—how could they?—would never be as beautiful as the afternoon they had just left behind.

When we finally took a seat it was in the shadow of a pillar that cast a protective shadow over the two of us.

"It's a good game," I said. "It always was."

"There really is nothing like sports," my father answered. "Don't let anyone ever tell you different."

And then, "You saw Jim O'Leary," my father said, less a question than a statement.

"Yeah," I answered. "He's retired now. He looked great. We watched part of a Giants game together."

"God, he loved baseball. So did you, especially when you were a kid. You wanted to be Daryl Strawberry when you grew up."

"If I couldn't be Magic Johnson first," I added.

"That's right," my father acknowledged. "The Magic Man was number one in your heart."

We both laughed.

"And your mother?"

"She's great," I said. "She's traveling through Europe right now."

"Is she still singing?" he asked.

"Once in a while. A friend of hers got married a few months back and she sang an old Paul McCartney song at it."

"The Beatles, eh? I could never get into those guys. But she loved them. We had a photograph of the four of them framed up above the sofa in our first apartment. Did you know that? You hadn't been born yet. We also had this TV where only one channel worked, some local access station that only showed televised jazz concerts. It was awful. And yet I don't think I was ever happier than I was in those years your mother and I spent in San Francisco."

"So tell me about this orphanage," I said, after a few moments' silence.

He looked off in the direction of the sunset, which gave the ancient ruins a divine glow of a kind I had never seen before.

"Nazim," he began, referencing his second wife, a lovely woman whose first husband had been killed during the Iran-Iraq War, "had a miscarriage about six years ago. It was strange. Suddenly I hit my early fifties and I wanted more kids. This seemed to be the best way," he said, nodding.

It was easy to forget that, for all of his wanderlust, my father had truly enjoyed so much of being a parent—especially the projects, teaching me to ride a bike, teaching me to swim, to play the guitar, to learn my multiplication tables.

"Anyway," he continued. "There are a lot of kids in this country who don't have parents. A real Lost Generation. I thought maybe rather than having one or two more of my own, I could help three hundred or four hundred instead."

"You always were ambitious," I said.

"That's the only way to be," he answered. "You know that as well as anybody."

After that we shifted into small talk, reminiscing about the first apartment we had lived in after I had been born, me telling my father about some of the guys I had gone to school with and what had become of them, catching my father up on the declining health of my mother's father, whom my father had loved deeply—"he remains the kindest man that I have ever met," he said—and about the current state of the Los Angeles Lakers, the franchise whose love my father and I shared so intensely that it saw us through some of the worst rough patches of our relationship.

An hour later we were back in a taxicab, heading for his house, which was located about forty miles away in Shiraz.

I stayed in Iran for three days. Long enough to meet Nazim (who apologized profusely for lying to me about my father's "death"), to visit the gravesite of the grandmother I had never met, to take a train-ride into Tehran to visit the Museum of Contemporary Art, a palatial establishment that houses enough Impressionist masterpieces to rival anything Western Europe has to offer, and to spend enough time with my father to remember why everyone, no matter how often he drove them crazy, loved him: the rules he played by were his own, but they were rules that he never changed, which meant that to be in his presence meant you were spending time with someone who was as authentic and as true to himself as anyone you were ever likely to meet. In other words, he was a man, the kind you rarely see anymore, and the kind that, once you've spent an hour in his orbit, changes your life for the better in an infinite number of ways.

The last night I was in Shiraz my father, Nazim and I all went to the Tomb of Hafiz. When I was three years old, for what my parents have later said was the first Halloween where I actually dressed up and went trick-or-treating, my father's choice for my costume was that of Hafiz: the photograph of me as the most famous of Persian poets is still on my mother's mantle. In it I am wearing a tunic that my grandmother had mailed from Iran for the occasion, and my mother had expertly penciled on a beard and thick eyebrows in order to complete the look. It's classic my parents, going as they did to great lengths for a costume that, truth be told, no one in America, especially no one in the apartment complex I grew up in, was going to understand. To every person handing out the assorted chocolate and peanut butter candies that were a staple of Halloween I was simply a strange little kid with a fake beard, a few individuals certain that I was a ghost who wanted to spice things up by putting on a little eyeliner. But whatever the case, that early costume did inspire a kind of subconscious connection to Hafiz that would later come to mean a great deal to me. My earliest poems, when, as a teenager, I would handwrite them into a little art sketchbook that belonged to my father in between episodes of *Happy Days*, were basically word-for-word rewrites of the Hafiz poems my father had been reading to me for years, and when my first book came out several years back, the collection's title was a line from one of my favorite Hafiz poems.

It was around eight-thirty in the evening when we arrived. It was still in the high 70s, and there were so many stars out that it looked less like an actual sky than one that had been imagined by Van Gogh. Of course, any sky on earth is going to shine more brightly than a Southern California one, where there is so much smog and diesel pollution that the state could be renamed The Asthma Capital of the World. But out here the stars were everywhere, the moon was the sliver that it so often is in old Disney fairy tales, when Mickey is dressed like a wizard and is sleeping on the back of a constellation as the entire world dreams along with him, and the reflecting pool was a deep, deep blue. On all the pillars were verses from Hafiz's most enduring gazals, and there were more people milling around—lovers sitting on the steps that led to the dome itself, children playing tag on the nearby lawn, old men gazing up in Gatsby-like wonder to the underside of the dome, where an arabesque of peerless beauty drew them into a trance-like state from which they would emerge renewed, if not literally reborn.

I don't think the three of us spoke at all. In fact, I'm certain that we didn't. What I do know is that it seemed fitting that my journey ended not with me standing in front of my father's tomb, but with the two of us standing in front of the tomb of someone else. Standing with my father at the Tomb of Hafiz felt like we had both come to bear witness, not only to pay our respects to a remarkable, and remarkably enduring, writer, but to pay our respects to mortality itself. It had always seemed like my father somehow stood outside of death, that through so many successive near-misses he had come to possess an insider-knowledge of death that he could now use to his advantage, and that night seemed to prove it. While all the other men assembled at the tomb that night were likely thinking, among other, more mundane things, that someday this too would be their fate, the look on my father's face was something else: it was one that knew he would never wind up like this. In my father's eyes was, truth be told, flat-out detachment. He knew he should feel something, but he simply couldn't. It wasn't arrogance that made him believe he was never going to die. It was something far more sensible: if it hadn't happened yet—and there had been so many opportunities—it simply wasn't going to.

After a minute he saw me looking at him and he met my eyes, shrugged, smiled, and said,

"Well, death isn't for everyone, you know?"

Five minutes later I was in a cab bound for the airport, and through the back window I watched as my father and Nazim stood holding hands beside the reflecting pool, maybe making wishes for the year ahead, or maybe saying a small prayer of thanks for the lives that had led them there. Whatever it was, it didn't really matter. It was a great last image to have of my father, who I would never see again: from where he stood, it looked like he was actually standing on the water, and looking down into the pool's depths with an almost palpable desire to know how it was he was doing it. It was the same look that my father used to have when I asked him about how he became as great as he had at soccer.

He couldn't, honestly, say. Everything in life is a mystery, the shrugging of his shoulders always implied, and the best we can do is embrace it.

About the Author

Paul Kareem Tayyar's previous books include *Follow the Sun: Poems, Stories, and Reflections* (Aortic Books), *Postmark Atlantis* (Level 4 Press), and *Scenes From a Good Life* (Tebot Bach). He lives in Southern California.

www.ingramcontent.com/pod-product-compliance
Lightning Source LLC
Chambersburg PA
CBHW020642250626
47154CB00008B/2775